THE
SPANIARD'S
KISS

THE
SPANIARD'S
KISS

NINA CROFT

Entangled Publishing
644 Shrewsbury Commons Ave
STE 181
Shrewsbury, PA 17361
rights@entangledpublishing.com

Amara is an imprint of Entangled Publishing.

Edited by Candace Havens
Cover design by LJ Anderson/Mayhem Cover Creations
Cover photography by Geber86/Getty Images

Manufactured in the United States of America

First Edition July 2015

For Rob—who made living in this fabulous part of Spain a possibility.

Prologue

"Bella?"

A squeak escaped her and she sank beneath the surface of the water. A second later, she came up spluttering. Blinking to clear her eyes, she pushed herself to her feet, wrapped her arms around her middle, and peered into the darkness. The moon had risen above the mountains, illuminating the tall figure standing in the shadows, and the tension eased out of her.

"God, Rafe, you made me jump."

He took a step forward, halting at the edge of the water, hands shoved in his pockets, a frown between his eyes. "What the hell are you doing out here alone?"

"Thinking." She shrugged. "I always come up here to think."

"Here" was a natural pool in the mountain up behind her house, formed where a thermal spring bubbled out of the hillside. The water remained warm even in January, and steam drifted up from the surface like tendrils of mist.

"Thinking about what?" he asked.

"Lots of things."

Moving on, mostly. Living in Spain had been her husband's dream, not hers, but Gary had been dead for two years now. It was time to stand on her own two feet and go after a few dreams of her own.

Her hand slid down to rest over the flatness of her stomach—one day.

"Come on out." Rafe's demand dragged her from her thoughts.

"Can't." She grinned up at him. "I've got no clothes on."

His gaze dropped, and his eyes narrowed. Her bare breasts were exposed, the water lapping at the tips.

She should retreat, or duck down, or tell him to go away. But honestly, did it matter that she was naked? Rafe probably wouldn't even notice. He'd be too busy lecturing her about the dangers of pneumonia. He'd never seen her *that* way. She would always be the wife of his dead friend.

He didn't speak again, just leaned toward her and held out his hand. Bella peered up into the hard, handsome planes of his face, his blue eyes almost black in the moonlight. No longer expressionless, they gleamed with an emotion she'd never seen in them before, and a prickle of unease ran over her skin.

Ignoring the sensation—this was Rafe, after all—she reached up, slid her palm into his, and allowed him to pull her from the water. Once on dry land, she tugged to free her hand, but his grip tightened. His focus remained fixed on her breasts, and they grew heavy, her nipples tightening.

Whoa.

What was going on?

Rafe had been Gary's best friend, now hers by default, and her goddamned nipples had no right to do anything in his presence.

Maybe it was just the cold air, and Rafe's staring was purely coincidental. Still, she wanted to tell him to let go, stop staring, make a joke that would get things back to normal, but her throat was dry and the words stuck.

When she didn't move, he reached out with his other hand, his fingers sliding beneath her hair, sure and firm, tilting her head toward him. He stroked the line of her jaw, the pad of his thumb grazing her lower lip, and all the muscles in her belly clenched tight.

Oh my God, he's going to kiss me.

It was inconceivable, but she couldn't move away.

Curiosity?

How far would he take this? Why was he taking it anywhere? And maybe more to the point—why was she standing here like a total moron and letting him?

The first touch of his mouth was gentle, but her lips tingled and shivers ran over her skin.

"Are you real or just my imagination?" he whispered against her lips.

She decided the question was rhetorical, and anyway, he didn't wait for an answer, just kissed her again. This time, his mouth slanted hard over hers, his tongue stroking across her lower lip. "Kiss me, Bella," he murmured.

His voice was low, like crushed velvet caressing her ears, drugging her mind, and for a moment she relaxed. Her mouth fell open, and his tongue pushed slowly inside, hot and wet, sliding against her own. Her body melted, growing heavy and unbelievably hot.

She almost protested when his lips left hers, but his warm breath feathered against her ear, distracting her. Then he was kissing her neck, lingering over the spot where her blood thundered close to the surface.

Any moment now he was going to pull away, turn back

into the old Rafe. And he was going to be *so* shocked, because she was naked, and he'd kissed her, and...

His hands slid down over her, leaving a trail of fire and turning her brain to mush. They settled for a moment on her waist, and then slipped around to caress the bare skin of her back and lower. He urged her toward him until the heat of his body warmed her through his thin silk shirt. The clean, masculine scent of him mingled with sharp, spicy aftershave filled her nostrils. She was drowning. Nothing had ever felt this good. Ever.

And that thought shocked her to hell and back. This was so not right. She tugged on his hair. "Rafe! Stop!"

For a second, his fingers tightened on her hips. Then he wrenched himself free and stepped back. "Shit."

Yeah.

He stood motionless for a second, hands fisted at his sides, damp shirt clinging to his broad chest. Then he exhaled loudly, leaned down, picked up her clothes, and tossed them toward her. "*Dios*, put something on."

She caught the clothes and dressed quickly. "Hey, don't sound so pissed off," she muttered. "You kissed me, remember. Not the other way around."

"Perhaps it's best we forget that ever happened."

Yeah, like that was ever going to happen.

Her lips still tingled from his kiss, her body flushed with heat. She opened her mouth to reply, but he'd already whirled around and was gone.

Bella stared after him.

Holy crap. Rafe had kissed her.

Like he wanted her. Really wanted her.

She hadn't seen *that* coming.

Chapter One

A pair of legs and an ass.

That was all Rafe could see, but it was enough to grab his attention, because the legs were long and slender and the ass full and curvaceous and barely covered by a pair of skimpy denim cutoffs. It was also pointed straight up at him where he stood at the first-floor window of his grandfather's villa. Rafe recognized her immediately, despite never having seen her from quite this angle before.

Bella.

The rest of her vanished into a dense green bush swathed in crimson flowers.

What the hell was she doing?

Her legs were golden brown, and her feet covered in thick woolen socks and heavy work boots. He didn't think work boots had ever entered into his sexual fantasies before. Scarlet stilettos were more his thing. An image flashed in his mind—a pair of four-inch heels on the end of those endless legs—and a wave of unwelcome heat washed over him, settling low in his gut. It had been a long time since a woman had affected him in this way. Six months, to be precise. Back then, it had been the very same woman, and the sensation had been just as unwelcome.

He still couldn't believe he'd kissed her. Something he'd sworn never to do. Bella was a friend; that's all she was, that's all she could ever be. He'd made the decision a long time ago, and Gary's death didn't change that.

The kiss had been a mistake of gargantuan proportions. But God help him, she'd been naked! Totally, gloriously naked. He'd spent most of the last six months trying to purge the memory from his mind. And failing.

A light tap at the door brought him back to the present. He shook his head and glanced around. Peter North, his assistant, stood in the doorway.

"How is he?" Rafe asked. His grandfather had been asleep when he'd arrived, and Rafe hadn't wanted to disturb him. He was awake now, but the doctor was with him.

"He's fine. As I told you on the phone—it was a minor attack."

Rafe had been in Hong Kong at the time and had headed straight back despite Peter's assurance that his grandfather was in no immediate danger. Probably his mad rush was due to guilt. He shouldn't have stayed away so long.

He worried about the old man; he was getting frail, and this place was too remote. Situated in the mountains between the Sierra Nevada range and the Mediterranean, the villa was a long way from the nearest hospital. Rafe had tried to get him to move to London where he'd be close to the best medical facilities, but his attempts were futile. His grandfather had lived here all his life and loved these mountains. God knows why—Rafe had never understood the attraction.

"Is the doctor finished?" he asked.

"He'll be done in five minutes."

"Good."

He turned back to the window and stood, hands in his pockets, observing the scene below. Peter came up beside him and whistled softly. "Nice."

Rafe stiffened. It *was* nice, but for some reason, he didn't like Peter sharing the view. Bella was hardly his property, but he still felt protective of her.

Protective. Yes. That was how he felt—he just had to keep reminding himself of that.

"What's she doing?" he asked.

"Pruning, I would think. She must be the new gardener your grandfather employed."

Rafe frowned. Why the hell would she be working as a gardener? He'd asked his grandfather to keep an eye on her, not to employ her. The old man would have looked out for her anyway. He'd been fond of Gary since he started coming here on holidays with Rafe when they were boys.

They watched in silence as she wriggled backward. It was a slow process, hindered by bits of bush that caught in her clothes and long, dark red ponytail. By the time she'd completely extracted herself, Rafe felt like some sort of voyeur, and Peter shifted uncomfortably beside him.

Scrambling to her feet, she brushed herself off, plucking broken twigs and crimson petals out of her hair. She still faced away from the window, and Rafe silently willed her to turn around. Finally, she turned so she stood in profile, and he ran his eyes hungrily over her. The skimpy shorts were topped by an equally skimpy khaki tank top that clung to the full curves of her breasts, leaving zero to the imagination and making it obvious that she wore nothing underneath.

Not that he needed imagination. He'd seen the real thing. *Dios*, why couldn't he delete that image from his head?

Protective.

His eyes shifted to her face. Her hair had grown since their last meeting, long enough to touch her ass, and she'd lost weight, but otherwise she looked the same—gorgeous.

"Her name's Isabel Sinclair," Peter offered from beside him.

"I know who she is—what's she doing working here?" Pete did security checks on all the new employees. He'd know the details.

"She's English—a widow with a small farm across the valley." Peter sounded nervous now, as though he wasn't sure what was going on. But then he'd only been with the company a year and would be unaware of Rafe's history with Bella. "I gather she's struggling to make ends meet. Your grandfather probably felt sorry for her."

Why was she struggling? He'd presumed Gary must have left her well off, but obviously not. And if she needed money, why the hell hadn't she come to him? That was something he could legitimately do for her, within the bounds of his protective role. Perhaps she hadn't wanted to ask him for help after that kiss. Maybe she thought he would demand something in return.

Not for the first time, guilt prodded him in the gut. Lately the emotion seemed to be a regular companion. Oh, she'd kissed him back—for all of about ten seconds—but probably because he'd taken her by surprise. She'd never shown any sign she saw him as anything other than her husband's friend, her friend. As far as he was aware, she'd never looked at any man other than Gary.

God, he was a bastard for kissing her.

The first time he'd seen her, eight years ago, was like being hit over the head with a blunt object. Hard. He'd wanted her from that moment. She was seventeen. Half tomboy, half siren. Rafe had been twenty-two, and he'd felt like a total pervert. She'd also been about to lose her virginity to the best friend Rafe had ever had. He remembered wishing that Gary hadn't confided in him quite so much.

Spending time with Bella had felt the same ever since— an almost painful blend of desire and guilt. He'd hidden his reactions and made sure he treated her like his kid sister. Lusting after his best friend's girlfriend, then wife, was not on his list of acceptable behavior.

But even if she hadn't been Gary's girl, no way would he get involved with her. Gary had told him all Bella wanted from life was a home and a family, and Rafe could give her neither. He'd grown up knowing those things would never be an option for him, and despite the money he poured into medical research, nothing had changed since then. He'd thought he was reconciled. He'd been wrong. Rolling his shoulders, he tried to ease the tension as an echo of remembered pain ran through him.

It had been easier when Bella was totally off-limits. He'd found the one woman he could imagine making a life with, and he couldn't have her. She belonged to Gary.

Except now, Gary was gone.

He'd done a good job of being Bella's "friend." Until that night at the thermal spring, when like a total moron—or more probably like a horny teenager who couldn't keep his dick in his pants—he'd kissed her. The memory still had the power to make him hot and hard.

The following morning, he'd discovered some urgent business demanding his immediate attention back in London. Okay—he was deluding himself. The truth was, he'd run away. And stayed away. Waiting for the memory of that kiss to fade. It hadn't happened. Then his grandfather fell ill and he'd hurried back.

He could get through this. As long as he didn't mention the kiss, they could return to the relationship they'd always had.

No problem.

• • •

He'd been gone six months. *Six months* and no word.

Snip. Snip.

She cut the head off a perfectly innocent geranium.

How dare he kiss her and then disappear for six months? Not that the kiss hadn't been nice—okay maybe "nice" was an understatement—but that was beside the point. He was supposed to be her friend. That's not how friends behaved. And he was only back because of his grandfather's heart attack. Who knew when he would have honored them with his presence otherwise? She'd missed him—hadn't realized how much she had come to rely on his sporadic visits.

Bella kept busy through the long morning, but by two o'clock, she'd pruned everything that could possibly be pruned. He wouldn't dare leave without seeing her, would he? She contemplated marching up to the house and demanding a confrontation, or tying herself to his helicopter so he couldn't leave without seeing her.

She wanted her friend back. That meant they had to face up to that kiss, show that it meant nothing, and get back to normal.

In the end, she convinced herself to wait until he approached her. But he'd better come quickly, or he'd be sorry.

Lifting her damp ponytail off her neck, she fanned herself.

She'd always loved the sun, but she didn't think she'd ever get used to the heat of a Spanish summer. Even sprawled under the dappled shade of a huge fig tree, where she could keep an eye on the main house, it was too hot to eat. Besides, her appetite was nonexistent, so she split the crusty bread between Sam and Joe, the two Doberman guard dogs sharing her shady siesta spot.

She'd done a lot of thinking since that night. Obviously, the whole naked thing had prompted the kiss. Rafe was a total player; she'd always known that. It was probably like Pavlov's dogs—the sight of a naked woman just triggered him to a sexual response. It was nothing personal.

And totally irrelevant that it had done all sorts of weird things to her insides. She was probably hormonal, and he'd had a lot of practice. He probably kissed all his women like his life depended on it, like he never wanted to stop.

And when she'd finally done the sensible thing and stopped it, he'd promptly vanished. She'd gotten up the next morning, determined to reassure him it meant absolutely nothing. But he'd already gone.

As the weeks turned into months, she came to suspect something—Rafe was avoiding her. But why?

Maybe he was worried she'd read too much into that kiss. Gary once told her that Rafe would never marry. He hadn't known why exactly, but it had something to do with Rafe's parents splitting when he was a boy. If he'd stuck around she could have put his mind at rest.

The kiss meant nothing. Absolutely nothing.

Yeah, she'd reacted, but he was a man, and she was a woman who hadn't been kissed in over two years. What did he expect?

And she could have used a friend to talk to. She'd thought about phoning him so many times, but something had always stopped her.

Sam raised his head from the ground, his growl quickly turning into a yip of greeting. Bella sat up abruptly.

"Crap," she muttered, as something hot and needy twisted low down in her belly. Had he always been that gorgeous? Or had that damn kiss rewired her brain?

Rafe strolled toward her across the vast expanse of green lawn, moving with the controlled arrogance of someone who owned the place. Which, of course, he did.

He was heading straight for her. At last.

Rafael Sanchez.

She'd first met him when she was seventeen, but she'd known about him for a lot longer. Rafe's and Gary's mothers had been best friends, and they'd grown up together.

Gary was three years younger than Rafe and had hero-worshipped him, talked about him incessantly. He'd been twenty-two and the most beautiful thing she had ever seen, with an air of raw sexuality she'd never encountered before... or since. All the same, it had never occurred to her to think of him as anything but Gary's friend and later hers. Maybe because he'd always treated her like an irritating kid sister. Besides, she'd known even then that one day she was going to marry Gary. She'd proposed to him when she was twelve and he was fourteen, and she'd never let him forget that he'd said yes.

As always, Rafe appeared cool and elegant in a pale gray suit and white shirt open at the throat. And as usual, Bella had to fight the urge to go over and muss him up, ruffle his hair, maybe leave some muddy fingerprints over his spotless silk shirt.

She scrambled to her feet and glanced down, taking in her bare legs, scratched and marked by mosquito bites, the tank top stuck to her damp skin. She'd also taken off her boots and was barefoot. She couldn't begin to imagine what she must look like, but she was 100 percent convinced "cool and elegant" didn't come close.

Rafe halted a few feet away, leaned one shoulder against the tree beside him, folded his arms over his chest, and regarded her from behind designer shades. "Bella, you look"—a slight smile curved his lips, and his gaze raked her from head to foot—"a mess."

What did he expect? She'd been working, it was hot, and, oh yeah, she hadn't been near a hairdresser in over two years. She didn't need Mr. Perfect, not a hair out of place, tall, dark, and handsome, to tell her that.

He was so unbelievably stunning. Well over six feet, broad at the shoulders but lean everywhere else. Immaculately cut black hair was brushed back from his face, his skin tinted with gold and drawn taut over to-die-for cheekbones. He reached up and took off his glasses, revealing the most sinfully erotic blue eyes she had ever seen. His lips were full with a sensual curve, and she had a flashback to the feel of his mouth on hers, his tongue—

"Earth to Bella...you can remember how to talk, can't you?"

Great. He was back to the old teasing Rafe. Did he honestly think he could pretend he hadn't kissed her?

Not in this lifetime.

They were getting this out in the open. Otherwise it would fester and ruin their relationship. She wanted her friend back. Unless he'd forgotten all about the kiss. Maybe he kissed so many women, and she was just one more.

She took a step closer, put her hands on her hips, and narrowed her eyes. "You *kissed* me."

Shock flashed across his features. No doubt he'd expected her to go along with him and not mention that night.

He pursed his lips. "It was a momentary aberration."

Her shoulders stiffened, her hands fisting at her sides.

How dare he call kissing her an aberration?

When she remained silent, he gave a casual shrug. "You were naked, I was distracted. It won't happen again."

That's right—put the blame on me.

She ground her teeth together. She'd see about that. "You kissed me, and then you ran away."

"I did not run away. I had to return to London."

"And you didn't come back."

"I've been busy."

"I can't believe you kissed me and ran away. Now you're trying to act like it never happened."

He took a step closer, picked up her left hand, and rubbed the gold wedding band she still wore. "It never should have happened."

"Gary is dead," she said. She could actually speak of her husband now without pain. That had taken a long time.

"I know. And I once promised him that if anything ever happened to him, I would look after you, make sure you're okay."

She frowned. "I'm quite capable of taking care of myself." *But that wasn't the point.* "How exactly would kissing me again make me *not* okay?" She didn't know why she was pushing this. Isn't that what she wanted? To get past the stupid kiss and move on?

"Right now, we're friends, Bella. Do you want to lose that?"

"Friends don't run away and hide for six months. And anyway, why would I?"

He ran a hand through his hair. "My relationships last about three months. I like variety. I'm never in one place for long, and I value my personal space. I'm not going to change."

"Jeez. Did I ask you to change? As it happens, I don't want a relationship."

She turned away for a moment to get her thoughts together, work out how to make this right. He was obviously putting way more importance on that kiss than she was. When she glanced back, she caught the first real expression on his face.

Hunger.

She clamped her lips closed before he noticed her shock.

As if he couldn't help himself, his gaze slid over her body, lingering on the curves of her breasts beneath the fitted top, and her traitorous nipples hardened to little peaks. Heat washed over her, and her bare toes curled into the grass.

Time to make a discreet exit while she considered strategy, but first, she had to be certain of one thing. "You're not going to do another disappearing act on me? You won't suddenly get called away by some vitally important paper clip that's gone missing, or some equally huge catastrophe?"

He shook his head. "I'll be here for a few days, until I'm sure my grandfather is okay."

"Good." Then she gave in to an urge, closed the space between them, and hugged him. "I missed you," she said, stepping back.

Not giving him a chance to answer, she turned around and headed off across the smooth green lawns feeling his eyes bore into her back with every step she took.

That evening, after she'd finished the jobs around the farm, Bella poured herself a glass of red wine and sat on the wooden bench in the garden to watch the sun set behind the mountains. Normally, this scene filled her with peace and had given her strength after Gary's death in a car accident, but tonight, nothing could settle her.

She'd known her husband since she was nine, and they'd married when she was eighteen, right after her dad died. She'd been alone, and they hadn't seen any reason to wait. His father hadn't agreed—he'd said they were both too young— but they'd done it anyway. A small service with only Rafe and Bella's best friend, Amy, as witnesses.

Then they'd moved to Spain and bought the farm. Partly because Gary had always loved the area, but also because

Spain was cheaper, and they could afford to buy the property outright. Bella had paid for the farm with money her father had left her, and they'd done the place up together. They'd been happy here, even if she'd been a little restless.

Draining her wine, she rose to her feet, crossed the garden, and opened the door to Gary's workshop, breathing in the lingering scent of cut wood. The place should have been cleared out months ago, but she'd never gotten around to it. She stepped inside and came to a halt beside the cradle Gary had been working on.

A familiar pain twisted her guts, and she slid her hand over her stomach. She'd been three months pregnant at the time of Gary's death, and a week later she'd lost the baby. Physically, she'd hardly suffered from the loss. Mentally, it had been like losing Gary all over again.

She stroked her fingers along the smooth wood and imagined a baby lying there, black tousled hair, eyes the color of the summer sky. The image stopped her short. Where the hell had that come from? Gary had been fair with gray eyes.

Staring at the cradle—the baby's image still clear in her mind—an idea began to take shape. A really bad idea that she recognized had been niggling at the back of her mind ever since that kiss.

A prickle ran up her spine and raised the hairs at the back of her neck. She turned slowly. Rafe stood in the open doorway, his tall figure outlined in the fading light. Heat washed through her as though he could actually see into her mind and her guilty thoughts.

She headed to the door and he stepped aside to let her leave. As she passed, she brushed against him, the contact sending a shiver rippling through her. Once outside, she turned to face him. "What are you doing here?" she asked.

"I wanted to make sure you were okay. You left so suddenly this afternoon."

"There didn't seem to be a lot to say. And I needed to think things through."

"And have you?" He sounded wary.

"Maybe." She'd come to the conclusion Rafe was definitely running scared. From her. It seemed impossible, but she could think of no other explanation. While he believed the kiss *had* been an aberration, he still wanted to do it again. He wanted her. And he wasn't happy about it.

"The kiss was a mistake," he said when she remained silent.

"Why? We're both single." She really wanted to understand where he was coming from with this. Was he worried she'd get all clingy? He should know her better than that.

He ran a hand through his thick dark hair. "Because we want different things out of life. You want marriage, children, and a home. I'll never marry, and I seldom stay in one place longer than a few days. We might have a fling, but then the differences would tear us apart. And you're too important to me for that. I don't want to lose your friendship."

Bella strolled to the table and poured a glass of wine. She held up the bottle to Rafe, but he shook his head. Taking a sip, she studied him over the rim of her glass.

She'd been trying to work out the details of her future. She needed a job, a career, but there was one thing she wanted above everything else. An image of that black-haired baby flashed in her mind. She thought of all she had lost, all that she now yearned for, and the really bad idea that had been floating in her subconscious crystallized into something tangible.

Rafe desired her. And that desire changed everything. It would be an honest exchange. A win-win situation. Placing her glass on the table, she took a deep breath. "You're wrong," she said.

"I am?"

She almost smiled at the wary note in his voice. She suspected not many people had the nerve to tell Rafe he was wrong. But she bit back the smile and nodded solemnly instead. "I'll never marry again."

His brows drew together as if he was trying to find the catch in that statement. She decided to help him out.

"No one will ever replace Gary. I don't even want to try—it wouldn't be fair. He was far more than a husband; he was also my best friend." And he'd left her like everyone else. No way would she risk that again.

"One day, you'll find someone else."

"No, I won't."

"Yes, you—"

She held up her hand to stop him before this got into a ping-pong match of an argument. "Believe me. *No one* will take Gary's place. But Rafe, there is something I want." She stepped close and tilted her head so she could look into his face. A tic jerked in his cheek. She placed her hand flat against the hard wall of his chest and felt the thud of his heart against her palm. Panic flared in his eyes, but he didn't back away. "Something I need," she continued. "Help me get it, and I won't ask for more than friendship from you."

The panic faded, and a smile curved his lips. "What do you need? You know I'll help you any way I can."

She suspected he might want to retract that statement any second now.

"I want your baby," she said, and watched as the smile slid from his face.

Chapter Two

"Who the hell is she talking to now?" Rafe growled.

He gritted his teeth as he stared down at the green lawn below the window. Bella was talking to a man. The man didn't look like much—middle-aged, medium height, dark-skinned—but even so, Rafe's hands balled into fists at his side.

She was wearing the same skimpy cutoff shorts as yesterday, this time topped with a white tank top. Rafe's eyes narrowed. The shirt bordered on indecent, almost see-through, clearly outlining the shape of her breasts. It didn't help that she had her hands shoved into the back pockets of her shorts, which had the effect of almost thrusting her nipples into the poor guy's face. Not that he appeared to be complaining.

Pete came to stand beside him. "That's Antonio Perez," he said. "The local shepherd. He's just been in to visit your grandfather."

At that moment, Bella laughed at something the man said, and Rafe's blood pressure soared until it pounded at his temples. "So what's he still doing here?"

"We did a full security check—he's quite safe."

Pete sounded puzzled. Rafe ignored it—he didn't pay his employees to be puzzled. "Is he married?"

"Yes."

Rafe grunted. "Good."

"And he has six children," Pete added.

That little piece of information set alarm bells ringing. The man was obviously stud material, and he'd bet Bella knew it. Why else was she flirting with him? What was she asking him down there? He could just imagine it—*I want your baby*. He turned to Pete.

"The man looks shifty to me, definitely a security risk. Get him off the property."

Pete opened his mouth and then sensibly shut it again. He didn't pay his employees to argue, either. Rafe watched as he left the room and then forced himself to move away from the window. Collapsing into the chair behind his desk, he ran a hand through his hair.

A dull ache throbbed behind his eyes, no doubt caused by lack of sleep and exacerbated by the onset of insanity. That was all it could be—Isabel Sinclair was driving him mad. It was two days since she'd made her preposterous proposition, and he hadn't felt entirely sane since.

Every time he turned around she was there—talking to some man. He hadn't realized there were so many men about, tall ones, short ones, fat ones, thin ones. Their appearance didn't seem to matter to Bella. Perhaps he should give her a little lesson in genetics, point out that she should be a bit more discerning if she was looking for someone to father her children.

His mind went back to that night. He'd reacted badly to her proposition. First, he'd accused her of wanting to trap him into marriage. Which was stupid. He'd never measure up to Gary in her eyes, but she'd caught him off guard and his mouth had overtaken his brain. She'd actually had the nerve to tell him that even if she had wanted to get married again—which she didn't—he would hardly be considered suitable husband material.

What was wrong with him?

He hadn't had to wait long to find out. She'd gone on to tell him he was immoral and a womanizer. She'd actually been nice about it, told him she didn't hold it against him—it was just the way he was. That he made a great friend, but she'd want other things in a husband. Dependability, responsibility, and faithfulness.

He was perfectly dependable. What did she know about it?

Actually, probably quite a lot, if Gary had talked to her as much as he had to Rafe. But no way was he a womanizer. He had a perfectly normal sex drive. His relationships might not last long, but they were always one at a time. Well, except for the twins. Christ, Gary hadn't told her about the twins, had he? Hell, what nineteen-year-old could have resisted that offer? Probably only Gary.

Rafe pressed his fingers against his eyes trying to ease the ache, and behind his closed lids he could see Bella standing there in her tiny shorts and equally tiny T-shirt.

He shifted in his chair. It felt as if his dick had been hard since their last meeting. And no relief in sight. If he had any common sense at all he'd leave that afternoon. Just get in his helicopter and fly away. His grandfather was well out of danger. Rafe should get back to London and find himself a nice willing woman. One who appreciated him. One who didn't fill him with such conflicting emotions that he felt as though his dick and his head might explode simultaneously.

But he couldn't do it. Common sense had deserted him along with his sanity.

Where the hell was Pete?

He got up, strode back to the window, and went instantly still. The shepherd was gone, but now she was chatting with Pete. Rafe jammed his hands into his pockets to stop himself from banging on the glass. Pete was single.

Pete turned to leave, and Bella reached out and put a hand on his arm. Every muscle in Rafe's body tightened.

I want your baby, she'd said to Rafe that night. But it was obvious that she wasn't bothered by whose baby she had. It occurred to him that he had a moral duty to warn his fellow men what she was up to. After all, nobody liked to be exploited. Though looking at her, he was sure most men would put up with being used to have that delectable body at their disposal.

She was obviously not yet over Gary's death or the miscarriage—the miscarriage had hit her hard. She'd wanted that baby desperately, and Rafe had been powerless to help her.

But it was also obvious she wasn't seeing clearly if she was willing to grab any guy just to get pregnant. She was young. One day, she'd find someone to love and have the chance for other babies.

Just not with him.

He ignored the pain that thought awoke inside him. There was no point wishing for what couldn't be.

He'd been eight when his father left his mother. They'd married when she was eighteen and pregnant with Rafe. His father had been a year older—a Spanish waiter working on the coast—and they should never have met in the normal course of things. She was sophisticated, loved the city. He was the son of a shepherd who longed for a simple life and the mountains.

His mother had wanted more children. His father hadn't. Rafe now understood there had been far more fueling their bitter quarrels, but that didn't change the fact that they loved each other, and it wasn't enough.

They said love conquered all, but Rafe knew firsthand what a load of crap that was.

His father had died a year after leaving, and his mother had remarried. She'd been happy with her second husband—he'd given her the lifestyle she'd wanted as well as four more children—but it wasn't a love match.

Rafe wasn't ready to settle for that sort of arrangement, either. So he stuck to relationships where the women wanted the same things he did. Mature, successful career women. Women absolutely nothing like Bella.

But it appeared Bella was going to do this baby thing, with or without him. She'd made that perfectly clear.

"Don't worry," she'd told him, shortly after the immoral womanizer comment. "Forget I mentioned it. There are loads of other men out there."

He ground his teeth at the memory of her words. He'd presumed she hadn't meant it. Now he wasn't so sure.

Could he stand by and do nothing while she went ahead with her plan with some seedy Spanish shepherd who already had six hungry mouths to feed? Or with Pete, who obviously didn't realize how close he was to instant dismissal?

It would be a grand dereliction of his promise to Gary to allow her jump into a relationship for the sole reason of procreation. So she had to be stopped.

She needed to get away from this place and from the memories, realize there were other things in life.

What if he gave her a tentative yes, but convinced her they should spend some time together before making such a momentous decision? Three months, and then they would see if she still felt the same.

If she did, he was fucked, because there were reasons he couldn't help her. Irrevocable reasons.

But hopefully, she'd come to her senses.

For the first time in two days, some of the tension eased inside him. He'd been fighting the inevitable, and it felt good to give in at last. He leaned against the wall and stared down at her, contemplated the pleasure of telling her that he was ready and willing to pay her price. But not just yet.

He was going to lie through his teeth, and all for a good cause.

• • •

Bella waited until Pete disappeared into the house before glancing up at the first-floor window. While she couldn't see inside, she could detect a small movement, and little prickles ran over her skin. Rafe was spying on her.

Again.

He was always watching her, which was having a disastrous effect on her behavior. She'd never before flirted in her life. If anyone had asked, she'd have said she didn't know how to flirt. Yet a few minutes ago, she'd actually found herself fluttering her eyelashes at Pete.

It was all Rafe's fault. She was pretty certain what he was thinking as he studied her. He thought she was chatting them up, making them an offer. The same one she'd made him.

How many times over the past two days had she considered marching up to him and telling him that her plea for help had been a joke? That she didn't want his baby?

But something stopped her. No doubt the same something that made her flutter her eyelashes at Pete and smile at poor Antonio, the shepherd, who had no clue why she was so friendly.

Because while Rafe might have ranted and raved, he hadn't actually said no.

She'd seen him yesterday, observing her as she talked to the doctor, suspicion clear in his eyes. What did he expect her to do? Leap on the old man and beg him to impregnate her? Bella almost laughed at the thought—the doctor was pleasant but was also nearing sixty. She'd actually been asking how Rafe's grandfather was. She was fond of the old man. The doctor had told her he was on the mend. Did that mean Rafe would leave soon? Go back to London? Who knew how long it would be before she saw him again? She sighed and returned to weeding the flower beds surrounding the vast turquoise swimming pool. Slipping on her earphones, she tried to convince herself to go tell him to forget she'd ever said anything. Reveal to him her plan to leave this place in the autumn, find a job, and build a career. She'd taken the position with his grandfather to save a little nest egg to keep her going until the farm sold.

Then she'd think about the other things she wanted from life. But she'd told Rafe the truth. She had no intention of marrying again. She'd loved Gary, maybe too much. She'd buried her dreams for him, because subconsciously she was terrified he would one day walk away like everyone else she loved. In the end, he hadn't walked away, but she'd lost him anyway.

A hand touched her shoulder, and she jumped. Pete again. "Rafe wants to see you," he said.

A shiver ran through her. Was that good or bad? "He does?"

Pete nodded, and Bella scrambled to her feet. As she followed him into the house and up the stairs, thoughts raced through her mind. What did Rafe want? Maybe just to tell her he was leaving. Or order her to stop flirting. Or... Deep in thought, she almost ran into Peter, who had stopped in front of the set of double doors leading to Rafe's office. He smiled at her encouragingly, tapped on the door, pushed it open, and gestured for her to enter.

The room was huge, with a bank of electronic equipment

down one wall. She hovered for a moment and then stepped inside, and the doors clicked shut behind her.

Rafe sat behind a large desk. He appeared relaxed, face expressionless, his dark blue eyes observing her steadily.

She forced herself to move closer, her boots clattering against the terra-cotta-tiled floor. Coming to a halt, she regarded him across the wide expanse of desk, and a flush of warmth heated her skin; a pulse throbbed in her throat. She tried not to squirm. This was like being back in school, hauled in front of the headmaster's desk.

Well maybe not quite like school, she couldn't help thinking as his gaze dropped from her face, over her breasts, down her legs. A slight smile flickered across his face as he took in her clumsy work boots. Then his eyes met hers.

"What?" she asked, her tone belligerent. "I do have important weeding to do."

He leaned back in his chair. "Okay."

Bella frowned. "Okay? Okay what?"

"You can have my baby."

Suddenly light-headed, Bella groped behind her to steady herself on the chair, then sank onto it because her legs refused to hold her any longer. She scrutinized him to see if he was joking, but he appeared serious.

"There's one condition," he continued.

"There is?"

"Only after we've spent some time together. I'm not convinced you've thought this through."

"I—"

"You were always impetuous. And stubborn. We need to take things slowly. I know you say you don't want marriage, but a child will bind us together more than any wedding ring. And there are legal and financial implications to sort out. I'll make adequate provision—"

"I don't want your money." She latched onto that.

"You have no choice. My child will not be brought up in poverty."

Bella's mouth opened, but nothing came out. She had what she wanted. Or did she? He was right—of course she hadn't thought it through. An image of a beautiful baby had flashed in her mind, and she'd jumped in with both feet. Rafe's baby. He was the closest thing to Gary she could get—they'd been like brothers. And he was her friend. If she wanted a baby, wasn't he the perfect choice? She clamped her mouth closed and stared at him.

A small smile curved his lips. "So, everything is agreed. I'm heading back to London this afternoon. You can close down the farm and join me there within the week."

"Join you? You mean live together."

He shook his head. "I don't live with anyone. I'll find you somewhere to stay to start with. If you want your own place later, then that's up to you. But I'll make sure we see each other."

She rubbed her finger between her eyes. Why did she feel like she'd lost control of the situation? Hah—when had she deluded herself she was in control? She took a deep breath. "So, let me get this straight…" Swallowing, she forced herself to go on. "I come over there and we 'see' each other. Just what does that involve? Will we…" She trailed off, not quite getting up the nerve to put the question into words.

"Have sex? Not until you're sure of what you want. We'll take things slowly."

"That sounds good." Actually, she'd prefer fast—get it over with—but that sounded a little…eager.

"Girlfriends are easy to come by," he continued almost gently, as if he was warning her of something. "Real friends are much harder. I've always believed we were friends. You need to be sure you're willing to lose our friendship if you go ahead with this—a baby will change our relationship."

The words shocked her almost more than his earlier agreement. She didn't want to lose his friendship, but she didn't see why that had to be the case—as long as they were both honest about their motivations.

"Rafe, do you want me?" she asked.

A tic jumped in his cheek, and she presumed he was going to deny it. "Yes."

Her mouth dropped open. "Oh." She thought for a moment how to word this. "And you've said your... relationships never last. So you get me, and presumably, by the time I get my baby, you'll no longer want me. We can go back to being friends with no nasty, bothersome sex to get in the way."

"Nasty, bothersome sex?" His tone held disbelief, and she had to clamp her lips closed to stop the giggle from falling out. Then he rose to his feet, and her urge to laugh did a runner straight out the door. He was so huge and intimidating. How had she never noticed before?

"Well"—she licked her lips—"I'm sure it won't be nasty. I'm sure it will be very...nice. After all, you've had a lot of practice."

His eyes narrowed, and that tic was on the go again. She sat glued to the chair, unable to move as he came around the desk, strolling with a languid grace that set her pulse throbbing in her veins. And something very inconvenient occurred to her.

She wanted him.

The need had been simmering under the surface since the kiss. She'd been doing her best to ignore it, but now every muscle in her body tightened as he came to stand in front of her. She kept her focus straight ahead, so she stared at his middle, somewhere around where his white shirt tucked into his black pants. He was so big, so masculine, and a fire flickered to life in her belly. For the first time, she considered exactly what they would have to do together to make a baby. Her eyes flickered lower, straying to the bulge in his pants, then she screwed them up tight. Swallowing the lump in her throat, she took a deep breath and thought about saying something.

"Don't you ever wear a bra?" he asked.

Her gaze flew up. His was focused on her breasts, and she fought the urge to cover them with her hands. They were already decently covered. "What?"

"A bra?" he repeated. "While I have to admit the view is very nice, it might be better if not everyone got to appreciate it."

Bella squirmed. "It's too hot."

"Hmm," he murmured, "you do look a little warm." His voice was low, husky, and a tremor ran through her. He leaned closer, reached out, and stroked a finger along her collarbone. "And you definitely feel a little on the hot side."

At his touch, the fire inside her roared to life, scorching along her nerves, and she was suddenly intensely aware of every part of her body.

Get a grip.

Wasn't he supposed to be the one doing the wanting?

From the flare of his nostrils, he must have sensed her reaction to him, and she needed to do something, anything, so he didn't have complete control of this meeting.

She opened her mouth to tell him she hadn't meant it in the first place. That she didn't want his baby after all. That he didn't have to worry about her. That she had her life under control. Before she could say a word, he leaned down and kissed her open mouth. Tingles spread from her lips throughout her body.

What was I saying?

He wanted to be friends and he'd kissed her. Maybe that was a "friendly" kiss. Though certain parts of her body were convinced his gesture meant more. Confused didn't begin to describe what she was feeling right now.

He straightened. "I'll have my lawyer set up an account," he said, his gaze dropping to her breasts again. "Buy some lingerie."

The conversation passed somewhere way over her head. How could she think about clothes when she could still taste him?

His eyes were focused on her mouth, and she was sure he was going to kiss her again. She might have even leaned in a little bit closer. Instead, he took a step back.

"You do look hot. Perhaps you should take a dip in the pool. In the meantime, I have to say good-bye to my grandfather. I'll see you in London."

He gave her one last comprehensive glance and strode out of the room.

Bella stayed in her chair for a long time, staring out of the window at the cloudless blue sky. At some point a door banged down the corridor, rousing her from her stupor. She blinked and looked around the study.

What have I done?

Could she somehow pretend the whole thing hadn't happened? She ran a hand across her forehead. Her skin was hot and damp, and she wiped away the sweat with trembling fingers. The room was cool, the air conditioner working, so why was she burning up? She must be coming down with something. In which case, maybe the last few days hadn't happened, and everything from the time Rafe returned had all been a figment of a fevered imagination.

Yes, that's it. I'm hallucinating. Kisses didn't feel that good.

Peeling her bare legs from the leather chair, she stood and wandered from the room, down the stairs, and out of the building. She hesitated, then turned and headed toward the pool.

She kicked off her boots and tugged off her socks. For a moment she stood poised on the edge, then she closed her eyes and fell face-first into the water.

Even the water felt warm. She wanted to sink, but rose to the surface. The clasp holding her hair in its plait came free, and long strands plastered her face and body. She swept it out of the way and blinked.

A pair of black shoes. Right in front of her eyes. She glared at them. It was hard trying to persuade herself they were part of the hallucination. They looked real. She prodded them with a finger—they felt real. Forcing her attention upward, she found Rafe staring down at her, a lazy smile lifting the corners of his sensual lips. She stared back, and warmth stole across her body, making the water cool by comparison.

"Hi," she muttered.

"You know," Rafe said, "most people take off their clothes when they go for a swim."

She scowled. "It was a spur-of-the-moment decision." Her eyes narrowed on him. "I thought you'd left."

He raised an eyebrow. "Obviously not."

"Oh." She must be coming across as real intelligent about now.

"I was with my grandfather." He gestured up to one of the first-floor windows overlooking the pool. "We saw you."

Bugger. "You did? Both of you?"

He nodded. "My grandfather was worried. I told him you were just cooling off, but he insisted I check to make sure you were okay."

"I'm okay. And since you were watching, it's probably a good idea I didn't strip." She pursed her lips. "Considering what happened last time."

He sucked in a breath.

Gotcha.

"By the way," Rafe said, "I've told him you'll no longer be working here."

Wow. This was really happening. "Please tell me you didn't mention the baby thing."

"I told him you'd decided to rejoin the real world and had asked for a job in London."

"And he believed you?"

Rafe shrugged. "Why not? He told me to tell you your job is here if you ever want to come back."

He reached out a hand to her. She looked at his long, tanned fingers, and then glanced down at herself. Even through the swirling water she could see the thin white tank top clinging to her body. Was his grandfather still watching? She ignored the hand.

"Actually," she said, with as much dignity as she could muster, "I think I'll swim for a little while longer."

Without waiting for an answer, she took a deep breath and dived.

When she finally came up for air, he was gone.

Chapter Three

How had she let things come this far?

Bella rested her head against the soft leather seats of the limousine and stared out the window, fingers clasped in her lap. They were driving through London, and as the city closed around them, a wave of panic spiraled up inside her.

"You have an appointment at the hairdresser's at ten tomorrow morning, then a meeting with your personal shopper at—"

Personal shopper?

"Please," Bella interrupted. "Stop right there."

She'd been listening to her companion drone on for the last half hour. Enough was enough.

"Is there a problem with your itinerary, Mrs. Sinclair?"

She cast the woman a sideways glance. She was around Bella's age, but that was the only similarity.

"Sorry," she said. "Just exactly who are you?" Bella was pretty sure the woman had introduced herself at the airport, but she'd been distracted at the time.

"I'm Sally—your PA."

"My PA?"

"Personal assistant. Anything you need, just let me know, and I'll sort it out."

Bella frowned. Did everyone think she was incapable of looking after herself? "I'm not helpless. I think if I need anything, I'm probably capable of getting it for myself."

She turned back to the window.

The past week had been surreal, everything organized for her down to her plane ticket and ride to the airport. Over the last two years, she'd become so used to coping on her own that the novelty of not having to think for herself had caught her by surprise, and she'd allowed herself to be carried along with the flow.

She'd considered putting the farm on the market, but in the end she'd decided she might need a hideaway if everything went to crap. So she'd closed the house up instead and asked her neighbor to keep an eye on the place. She'd sell it in the autumn as she'd originally planned, though she was trying not to think about that too much. The place had so many happy memories. But she'd need the money. Finally, she'd said her good-byes, and managed to avoid thinking about the future and what she was doing.

Then she'd boarded the plane. As she settled into her luxurious first-class seat, she'd been engulfed by a wave of panic so intense it would have brought her to her feet had she not been securely fastened in. The following three hours had dragged with nothing to occupy her but thoughts of Rafe and the deal they'd made.

Why had he agreed? After the kiss, she'd believed he wanted her. But the more she'd thought about it, the more her crazy brain had convinced her that she was totally deluded. She'd known him for so many years, and he'd never shown even a glimmer of interest.

Was this some kind of misguided loyalty to Gary? Was

this just another way of looking after her? Had she actually convinced him she'd have a relationship with anyone just to get a baby? Surely he knew her better than that.

By the time they started the descent into London, she'd come to her senses. She'd tell him the deal was off, and they could have a good laugh about it. Then with any luck she'd be able to get a flight straight back to Spain. She could lick her wounds for a little while and then go back to her original plans.

A plea of temporary insanity was her best bet, and she practiced the words she'd say to Rafe, running them through her mind over and over again.

What can I say? I'm crazy? Sorry for the inconvenience...

Except when she disembarked from the plane, he wasn't there.

Instead, she'd been met by little Ms. Efficiency, with her smart gray business suit and matching briefcase. And despite the fact that Bella had been about to tell Rafe she'd rethought the whole thing, a wave of very unwelcome disappointment engulfed her at his absence.

Engrossed in trying to analyze her feelings, somehow, she'd ended up in the back of a limousine heading through London. Now all this talk of hairdressers and PAs was doing her head in. Why the hell would Rafe set her up with a PA?

"Can I look at that?" Bella reached for the tablet computer. For a moment, Sally's fingers tightened, and it looked like they were about to descend into an undignified scuffle in the back of the limo. Bella raised one eyebrow, and the other woman relinquished her hold, albeit with obvious reluctance.

She ran her eyes down her "itinerary." "Is he crazy?" she asked. "I'm not doing all this stuff." She thought for a moment. "Did Rafe say I needed all this?" She wasn't perfect, and he had said she was a mess, but it sort of hurt that he'd want to change her so drastically.

"No. He just told me to organize some things for you. But he did mention you'd been living in the middle of nowhere and you might enjoy some pampering and so on."

Would she? She'd never been pampered before. Neither her father nor Gary had been the pampering type. But that was beside the point. Bella handed the tablet back. "I don't think so."

"What about the personal shopper? Mr. Sanchez was adamant you'd want clothes."

Bella glanced down at herself. She was dressed in her best jeans, maybe a little threadbare but no actual holes, her work boots, a T-shirt, and one of her dad's old army shirts, with its sergeant's stripes, over the top. Not glamorous, but perfectly adequate. And while she did need to sort out some new things for when she went job-hunting, that wasn't the point.

"I don't want Rafe buying me anything."

"Actually, there's already quite a lot of stuff at the hotel. It started to arrive a couple of days ago." Sally tapped something into the tablet before looking back at Bella. "You know, you should feel honored. Mr. Sanchez is a busy man."

"Hmm. 'Honored' isn't quite the word I would use."

Confused. Disoriented. Insane.

Bella regarded the other woman curiously. "Do you do this often?" she asked. "I mean, is this like a full-time job— looking after Rafe's...girlfriends?" She wasn't actually his girlfriend, but explaining what she was would take way too much time.

"No, this is the first time. I work in the office. I'm sort of PA to Mr. Sanchez's PA."

"Why do I get the special treatment?"

Sally looked at Bella over the top of her tablet, and for the first time she grinned. "You're not much like his usual girlfriends."

"I bet," Bella muttered. "So what are they usually like?"

"Sophisticated, perfectly groomed, glamorous—"

Everything I'm not.

Bella held up a hand. "Okay, enough." But she couldn't resist one more question. She'd always been curious about Rafe's love life—it was just so...prolific, and he'd usually told her to mind her own business when she'd teased him about it. "I bet they're all supermodels and actresses, aren't they?"

"Actually, no. Mr. Sanchez prefers more mature, successful career women. The last one was a criminal lawyer—quite scary." She frowned. "Though she was over a year ago now. Maybe his tastes have changed."

"Really?" The information surprised her, though why, she didn't know. Sighing, she gestured to the tablet. "It's not going to happen, you know."

"Not even the clothes?"

Bella shook her head.

"I'll probably get the sack," Sally said.

"I'll tell him it's not your fault."

"Thank you. That reminds me..." She opened her briefcase and took out a phone. "I've put Mr. Sanchez's number on speed dial, but I suggest you only phone him in absolute emergencies. Mr. Sanchez is a—"

"—busy man. I got that bit."

Bella took the phone and stared at it for a moment. She would have preferred to do this face-to-face and without an audience. But if she got through to him now, there was still time to turn the limo around and go straight back to the airport. She hit speed dial. It rang a couple of times before it was picked up.

"*Querida.*" The voice was low, husky, and instantly recognizable. He'd never called her *querida* before. Why would he? Did he know it was her? Or was this the number he gave to all his girlfriends?

"It's Bella," she said, just in case.

He chuckled. "I know."

Now that she had him, she wasn't sure how to start. "Did I interrupt anything?"

"Nothing important. I was asleep."

Bella frowned. "You're in bed?"

"That's where people usually sleep."

"But it's only seven o'clock." Wasn't he supposed to be a busy man?

"Not in Hong Kong."

He was in Hong Kong? It was half a world away. She gripped the phone tighter in her hand, not sure what to say next. Closing her eyes, her mind instantly filled with an image of Rafe sprawled across black silk sheets like some sort of *Playgirl* centerfold. She opened her eyes, took a deep breath.

"So you're in bed, then?" *Stupid question.*

"*Si, querida*—dreaming of you." She heard a faint thread of amusement running through his voice. "Do you want to know what I'm wearing?"

She thought for too long about her answer—before the words left her mouth, he continued.

"*Nada*." His voiced dropped to a low murmur. "Nothing," he added, obviously in case she didn't understand. Or maybe he was just trying to fluster her or frighten her off. In which case, he was doing a hell of a good job. Time to tell him he didn't need to bother—she'd managed all on her own.

"Really?" She tried for cool and failed. The sound of his soft laughter caressed her sensitive ear. Even his laugh was sexy. How had she never noticed that before? Shivers rippled through her body, and she squirmed on the leather seat. A small sound from beside her reminded her she wasn't alone. This was so not the right time to start acknowledging Rafe's sexy side. She doubted there would ever be a right time for that.

She glanced across at Sally. The other woman was staring out of the window, her fingers drumming on the edge of the tablet clutched tight to her chest.

Time to take control of the conversation. "Look," she said to Rafe. "I'm sorry I woke you."

"I'm not. So, q*uerida*, are you alone?"

She shook her head. Then realized he couldn't see her. "No, actually I have my new PA with me."

"Get rid of her."

"Not really an option unless you want me to toss her out of a moving vehicle."

He sighed down the phone line. "I'm sorry I wasn't at the airport. I meant to be there, but I was delayed."

"You did?"

"Yes, but I'm coming back tomorrow."

"You are?"

"I fly back first thing in the morning."

"You do?"

"*Si*. Now I suggest you let me rest and I'll see you tomorrow."

"You will?"

"I will. Good night, q*uerida*."

She heard the *click* as he disconnected. For a moment, she sat with the phone still pressed to her ear. Then she placed it gently on her lap and rubbed her forehead.

Well, that had gone well.

"Sexy" Rafe was messing with her head.

What had happened to "taking things slowly?" And "just being friends?" Obviously, she wasn't the only one a little confused about where they were going with this "relationship."

She turned to look at Sally, who stared back at her, wide-eyed. Bella ignored the look, took the tablet from the other woman's hands, and fanned herself.

"Hot in here, isn't it?"

• • •

What the hell was he doing?

He rubbed his forehead to ease the exhaustion and jet lag tugging at his brain. If he had any sense, he'd be heading back to his house and his own bed. Somehow it hadn't worked out that way, and he found himself instructing his driver to take him to Bella's hotel.

Traveling through the silent streets, he pondered the long and entirely unproductive conversation he'd had with his lawyer on the phone that morning. John was a friend as well as his legal adviser, and he wasn't happy with this baby deal. And Rafe couldn't tell him that the whole thing was a ruse and he had no intention of having a baby with Bella. With anyone, for that matter.

He'd gotten the impression John thought he was going through some sort of premature midlife crisis. That he needed a child to fulfill him, or leave everything to, or…

John had gone to great lengths to warn Rafe of the repercussions of allowing a woman to have his baby and latch onto his life and his money. He was right. Not the money—Bella didn't have a mercenary bone in her body. But pretending he could give her a baby had been a moment of madness. He had no right to lead her on with promises he'd never fulfill. He could see that now.

While she'd said they were making an honest exchange— her body for his sperm—he was actually being far from honest. But he couldn't let her go through with that with someone else. He'd promised Gary he'd look after her, but it was more than that. The need to protect her drove him, and every instinct screamed she was making a huge mistake, moving too fast in an attempt to fill the void left by losing Gary and the baby. But there were other things in life, and perhaps spending time in the city might help her remember there was a great big world to explore, and he was more than willing to be her guide.

He sighed. He'd talk to her, explain he'd had a rethink and the whole thing was impossible. She'd hopefully reached the same conclusion herself. She wasn't stupid—far from it.

Pushing the key card into the lock, Rafe paused. He stared at the closed door. It was three in the morning.

He really shouldn't be here.

Control was slipping away from him along with his sanity, but since he'd spoken to her yesterday, he hadn't been able to concentrate on anything else. Also, he was feeling uneasy about that telephone conversation. He was supposed to be keeping their relationship strictly friendly, and he suspected he might be sending out a few mixed messages. But she'd caught him unawares, woken him from a particularly vivid dream…

He'd just check that she was okay, that she had everything she needed and wasn't homesick.

Had she missed him? Purely as a friend, of course.

His flight had been delayed again because of weather. Normally, such delays didn't faze him. He just used the time to catch up on work, but today he'd been too keyed up to concentrate.

Closing his eyes, he imagined her waiting for him just on the other side of this door, and a rising sense of anticipation banished the exhaustion clouding his brain.

He pushed the door open and dropped his overnight bag on the floor. He didn't switch on the light. No doubt at this hour she'd be asleep, and he didn't want to disturb her. He'd just check to make sure she was okay and then catch a nap on the couch. After tapping lightly on the bedroom door, he eased it open and stepped inside. The room was dominated by a massive four-poster.

A massive *empty* four-poster.

He frowned, reached over, and switched on the lamp. There was definitely no beautiful woman curled up sleeping, and a stab of something hit him in the gut. Disappointment? Worry? The new and unexpected feelings gave him pause.

Where the hell is she?

He glanced around the room. The place was littered with clothes and shoes, empty bags and boxes spilling their contents over every available surface as though some sort of mini tornado had hit. He picked up a scrap of black silk and lace, and then tossed it down. He hadn't ordered this much stuff. Had he? He'd never in his life bought clothes for a woman before—it had been a new experience—and perhaps he'd been carried away.

He had a notion that perhaps "friends" didn't buy each other underwear, but he pushed the thought aside. They were just a welcome-back-to-England present. Bella didn't need to know that he'd been unable to stop his imagination running rampant when he envisaged her wearing them.

He tried the bathroom door; it opened, but there was no one inside.

Where was she?

Doubt nagged at his mind. She wouldn't leave, would she?

He flicked off the lamp, left the bedroom, and returned to the sitting area, this time switching on the main light. He saw her straightaway, curled up on one of the huge scarlet sofas. An empty bottle of wine and a glass stood on the coffee table beside her, with a big red-and-white paper tub labeled "popcorn" next to it. He peered in—it was also empty.

Rafe moved to stand over her. Enveloped in one of the hotel's fluffy white robes, she was covered almost completely, though he could see one bare toe peeking out from where her feet were tucked under a cushion. Her arms wrapped around a second cushion, and her long red hair was loose, obscuring her face. He crouched beside the sofa and reached out, stroking the hair back, and something twisted inside him. She'd been crying. Tears stained her face, and a wave of some unidentifiable emotion flooded over him.

He wanted to take her in his arms, comfort her. Instead, he rubbed the pad of his thumb across her cheek as if to wipe away her sadness along with the tears. Her face was bare of makeup, her lush pink lips slightly open, and desire stirred to life low down in his body. He gave in to the urge, leaned in close, and kissed her briefly, tasting the sweetness of toffee popcorn on her lips. She didn't wake, but rolled onto her back and hugged the cushion tighter to her chest.

"Gary?" she murmured.

Rafe's hand dropped away as though he'd been burned.

Gary wouldn't be against a relationship between them, but Rafe had felt guilty about his desire for this woman for so long, it was impossible to turn off.

He stood abruptly as exhaustion washed over him. He needed a shower and a bed. Instead, he shrugged out of his jacket, tossed it onto the back of the sofa, and sank into the chair opposite where he could watch her sleep.

• • •

Bella blinked. Something woke her. She ran a hand through her hair and then rubbed her eyes. The light was on. She was sure she'd turned it off, but her brain was fuzzy.

The empty wine bottle probably had something to do with that.

She hadn't been able to eat all day. The tight knot of excitement in her belly made the idea of food impossible.

Then Rafe's assistant had phoned, told her Rafe wouldn't be back, and she'd deflated.

The hotel suite was luxurious. This might have been the one and only time she stayed in a place like this, so she decided to take advantage.

She'd wallowed in a long bubble bath in the extravagant bathroom, dressed herself in one of the complimentary robes, and called room service. A bottle of wine, a tub of popcorn, and one of her favorite weepy movies.

She should go to bed—it was after three in the morning—but that would mean clearing all the stuff away. The amount of clothing he'd bought was unbelievable, and absolutely none of it any use for the future. Slinky nightwear, flimsy underwear, even a pair of scarlet stilettos she hadn't taken from the box, though her fingers itched to touch them.

Did he make a habit of buying stuff like this for his friends?

Something caught her eye. Turning her head, she stared at the black jacket stark against the crimson of the sofa. It hadn't been there before, and her heart rate picked up. She forced herself to relax. Where was he?

She looked around the room and couldn't believe she hadn't seen him immediately. He was seated on an armchair opposite her, long legs stretched out, head back against the seat, eyes closed. His glossy black hair fell over his forehead. There were hollows beneath his cheekbones, and his sensuous mouth was relaxed in sleep. Awake, there was a hardness to him, a sense of invulnerability. Now his features were softened, and she had an urge to go hug him. But Rafe wasn't the hugging type.

He wore a white shirt with a maroon tie, loosened at the neck, and dark pants. Her eyes lingered on the long, lean length of his body, then moved back up to his face. He was awake, his eyes gleaming behind half-closed lids.

Sitting up, he ran a hand through his hair, tousling the perfect cut. "You were dreaming about Gary. You said his name."

Bella shook her head, trying to clear her mind. For more than a year after Gary's death, she'd dreamed of him most nights. Horrible dreams that she woke from to abject misery. But she didn't feel miserable now. Her heart was racing, her mouth dry. "Really?" she said. "I don't remember."

He studied her as if she wasn't what he expected. "And you were crying," he said after a minute's silence. The words sounded like an accusation.

She wiped her cheek as though she could remove the evidence. "I was watching a movie. It was sad—you know I always cry at sad movies. Anyway, I didn't expect you tonight."

"My plane was delayed."

"I know. Your assistant phoned."

What was he doing here? What did he want?

She was alone in a hotel room, in the middle of the night, with a man she had positively begged to make love to her. Well, maybe "making love" wasn't the right term. Donate sperm? Not nice.

A man whose hot, hungry eyes were eating her up.

She hadn't been deluded.

He wants me.

Her mind froze while her body heat rocketed, sweat prickling her skin.

She was still hugging a cushion to her chest, and she tossed it to the sofa and rose to her feet, pulling the robe tighter around herself.

His gaze followed the movements. "Did you miss me today?" His voice was like warm, sticky honey, and the heat concentrated low in her body.

Whoa. What was that?

Not part of the deal at all. She swallowed and moistened her dry lips.

What was the right answer? Yes? No?

He rose gracefully to his feet. Holding her breath, she waited for him to move, but he stood looking down at her. "There's something I need to discuss with you," he said.

"Can't it wait until tomorrow?" An overwhelming urge swept over her. To reach out and touch him, stroke her finger along his cheek.

Bad idea. Crazy idea.

Crazy or not, of its own volition her hand brushed the rough skin of his jaw. He leaned into her caress, and heat licked along her nerves, coalescing at her nipples, between her thighs.

Danger. Danger. Danger.

Her mind screamed, but her hormones were not in agreement.

Traitorous hormones.

Taking a deep breath, she forced her hand to her side and shoved it into her pocket.

No more touching.

But she could look. For the first time, she noticed the shadows under his eyes. "You look tired."

"It's been long day."

"Why don't you go have a shower and get some sleep? You can stay here tonight—there's plenty of room."

His eyes narrowed. "There's only one bed."

"It's a big bed." The words sort of fell out of her mouth, and she had no clue why. Or maybe she did. She felt alive, more alive than she had since…well, since he'd kissed her that night at the pool.

He glanced toward the bedroom door and took a step back as if to distance himself. Almost as if he were scared. The idea was so far-fetched it broke the tension, and she grinned. "Come on, Rafe, I promise your virtue is safe with me."

He rolled his shoulders. "A shower would be good—I feel like I've been traveling for days. But I'll take the couch." He nodded to the sofa she'd been sleeping on.

Bella shrugged. "Your choice, but I think I can manage to restrain my lust."

"Maybe we should avoid the temptation," Rafe said. "You go to bed. I just wanted to check that you were all right, and we can talk in the morning." Then he was gone.

Her body thrummed with tension, her skin flushed and sensitive. Lowering herself back onto the sofa, she contemplated the door where he'd disappeared and finally admitted it to herself.

Crazy or not. She wanted him

Would it be such a bad thing? They were both single. Who would it hurt?

The water started running, and she chewed on her lip as she imagined Rafe in there, naked, wet, all slippery with the soap…

• • •

He dried himself after the shower and then realized he'd left his overnight bag in the other room. Wrapping a towel around his middle, he opened the door and peered out. There was no sign of movement from the bed. He silently crossed the room and into the living area. And stopped.

Bella was perched on the edge of the sofa, still in the robe. She glanced up as he came out of the bedroom, and her eyes widened.

"Holy crap," she muttered, her eyes glued to his naked chest. "Okay, I lied. Maybe I can't restrain my lust after all."

She rose slowly to her feet and fiddled with the end of her

belt. Then she clamped her teeth on her lower lip, pulled the robe open, and pushed it off her shoulders. It slipped to the floor and left her standing before him naked.

She was perfect, everything he remembered from that moonlit night. "Bella," he groaned.

Why was she doing this to him? There was a look in her eyes, half hopeful, half scared, and he realized how much courage that action had taken. Obviously she wasn't sure of him. Which was crazy. She only had to glance down to where his dick pushed at the towel to know the effect she had on him.

Then she did glance down, and he heard her sharp indrawn breath. She raised her head to stare into his face. "I think we should do this."

The simplicity of the statement was so like Bella. Always direct and honest. No subterfuge. He didn't have the willpower to walk away.

He'd probably been beaten the moment he'd decided to stay. Or maybe the moment he'd told his driver to bring him here. Maybe even when he'd agreed to her ludicrous proposal. It didn't matter. A wave of inevitability washed over him.

It was too late.

He closed the distance between them and scooped her into his arms.

Chapter Four

"Ow," Bella squeaked as he dropped her on the mattress.

"What is it?"

Instead of waiting for a reply, Rafe flipped the switch on the lamp. Warm golden light filled the room. Bella lay on the bed, naked, amid a pile of clothes, boxes, and bags. Rafe swept the whole lot onto the floor, littering the place with lace and satin, then stood back to take her in. She was beautiful, with the perfect long lines of a thoroughbred and full breasts tipped with tight pink nipples. The curls between her slender thighs were dark red to match her hair.

A shaft of heat shot straight to his groin. "You're beautiful," he said, his voice rough with need.

The towel was still wrapped around his waist, and he tugged at the knot and tossed it to the floor amid the rest of the clutter. Her gaze dropped to his erection, and her eyes widened.

He came down on the mattress beside her and ran a hand along the length of her body, the swell of her breast, the smooth indentation of her waist, the jut of one hip bone.

"I want you," he whispered, burrowing his face against her throat, breathing in the scent of jasmine that clung to her skin. He kissed her quickly. Then a quick kiss wasn't enough, and he parted her lips with his, pushed his tongue inside her mouth, tasting her sweetness.

Her tongue moved tentatively against his, velvet soft, and blood pulsed in his groin.

She was perfect, her breasts small but full, the tips dark against her golden skin. He grazed the pad of his thumb over one swollen nipple, and she moaned low in her throat.

Unable to resist, he leaned closer and swiped his tongue over the peak, then watched it pucker and tighten. He took it between his lips and sucked, feeling her hips jerk against him.

Needing to be over her, inside her, he dragged her into his arms and beneath him, so his shaft nudged at the entrance to her body.

The wait was nearly over.

With one hand, he reached for a condom from the cabinet beside the bed.

Then remembered.

Shit.

No condoms.

It was like being doused in cold water.

Of course he had no condoms, because he never intended for this to happen. He rolled onto his back. How the hell had it happened?

Bella pulled the edges of the sheet around herself and sat up, her expression dazed, but coming around. "What is it?"

"We can't do this—no condoms."

She placed a hand on his chest over his heart, and he fought the urge to run. "We don't need condoms—"

Yes, they did. Rafe just wasn't sure how to tell her. "That thing I wanted to talk to you about? I was going to tell you I made a mistake. I should never have agreed. The whole baby thing was a terrible idea."

"So why am I here?" She blinked, an expression of bewilderment crossing her face, her brows drawing together. "I can't believe this. Why didn't you tell me earlier, like before I got on that plane yesterday?" She tugged the sheet up higher, fingers clutching the material. "But you're right. It is a terrible idea. I'll go back to Spain in the morning."

The hell she would.

He ran a hand through his hair. Opened his mouth, closed it again. He had nothing to say that made any sense right now. Instead, he pushed himself off the bed. He had to get out of there. "I have to go. But I promise to explain tomorrow. Please don't leave until we talk."

He kissed her quickly, ran a finger along her jaw, and hoped she would listen to him. At least this once.

He turned around and strode from the room. It would have been a grand exit, except he tripped over a scarlet stiletto and nearly landed on his ass.

"Shit! Crap, that hurt." Still cursing loudly, he picked himself up and headed for the door.

• • •

Bella waited to hear the slam of the door as he left the hotel suite, but all was silent. Then she realized he couldn't leave without coming back through there—his clothes were in the bathroom. But he didn't return, and she sat hugging her knees to her chest for what seemed like an age.

Well, that had gone well. Not.

He'd definitely been about to give in. She might not be experienced, but he'd wanted her. It was pretty hard to hide an erection that big. Then he'd ruined it. No doubt they were back to the "friends" thing.

She stretched out and plonked her head on the pillow,

tried to wipe the memory of his touch from her mind. But it had felt so good. She hadn't realized how much she had missed physical contact with another human being. How lonely she had been. But maybe it was for the best.

All through her childhood, she'd never belonged anywhere. Most of her childhood had been spent at boarding schools arranged by the army. Marrying Gary and moving to the farm had been all she'd ever wanted. A place where she wouldn't have to move on every few months or years. It hadn't worked out like that. She'd ended up alone anyway, and now she was moving on once more. She hadn't given up on the dream of belonging. She just wasn't prepared to risk putting her happiness in anyone else's hands again.

She tossed and turned, her ears tuned for any noise from the next room. Finally, she slid off the bed and tiptoed to the doorway. The sitting room was in darkness except for the glow from the bedroom lamp filtering through the door, but she saw him easily. He was lying on the sofa in her white robe, fast asleep. His face had that slightly vulnerable look again. Dark lashes shadowed his hard cheekbones, and his stern mouth was softened, revealing the sensual lower lip.

Warmth stole over her that had nothing to do with sex. She had to fight the urge to wrap her arms around him, tell him everything would be all right. It occurred to her that despite his family, he was just as alone as she was. But then he'd always said he was closer to Gary than he was to any of his real family.

Why was he so adamant that he'd never marry? Presumably something to do with his family, who sounded as messed up as her own. Funny how their similar pasts had sent them in totally different directions. She was determined to get the home she'd never had, while he swore he'd never settle down.

Reluctantly, she dragged her gaze from his still form and

returned to the bedroom, shutting the door firmly behind her. There was no lock, but she didn't think Rafe would be back.

Crawling under the covers, she curled into a ball and eventually fell into a restless sleep.

• • •

Rafe awoke to the disturbing feeling there was something not quite right with his world. Daylight was just beginning to filter through the curtains. He glanced at his watch; it was before six, and he groaned and sat up slowly.

He had a crick in his neck and was cuddling a scarlet cushion to his chest and wearing a fluffy white robe.

The fabric smelled of Bella.

And the whole fiasco came back to him. He glanced over at the bedroom door, but it was firmly closed.

Shit.

He'd made a total fuckup of last night. He put it down to exhaustion and incipient madness caused by her naked body. Control and good intentions flew out the window when confronted by a naked Bella. He was only human.

The bewilderment in her eyes killed him.

Massaging his scalp, he tried to imagine her on a plane returning to Spain that very morning. His gut tightened. No. He wouldn't allow it. If she went back now, what would she get up to? And whom would she get up to it with?

Anyone other than him just wasn't an option.

No, he had a duty to keep her out of trouble, and that meant keeping an eye on her for the foreseeable future.

But he didn't want to take advantage of her, and he didn't trust himself. From now on, he'd steer clear of any situations where a full set of clothes wasn't an absolute necessity.

How do I get things back on track?

He had to offer some gesture to reassure her that he

wasn't just out for a quick shag.

The contract.

Get the whole thing down in writing. Convince her he meant business. Then she'd have to believe his sincerity. Maybe.

His jacket was still over the back of the sofa, and he reached into the pocket and pulled out his cell phone. He punched in a number and waited for the sleepy reply.

"John, I want you to draw up the papers."

"What papers?"

"The baby papers we talked about. I want them in my office by ten this morning to go over."

He switched off before he had to listen to John's arguments again. They were valid only if he had any intention of going through with the baby deal.

And that couldn't happen.

Some of his tension drained away. He stood and stretched, then headed to the bedroom.

Bella lay in the center of the bed completely covered, only her dark red hair showing against the white pillow. He tiptoed to the bathroom, found his pants and shirt, and pulled them on, then returned to the bedroom. He wanted to get this conversation over with and get his plan back on course.

He sank onto the bed and touched her lightly on the shoulder, or where he presumed her shoulder would be under the covers. She snuggled down, murmuring something. If she called out another man's name now, he might explode. He took a deep breath and shook her this time.

Her head rose from the pillow, and she smothered a yawn with her hand. "Is it time to go to the airport?"

"You're not going to the airport."

Her arched brows drew together. "I'm not?"

"We have a meeting with my lawyer at eleven."

"We do?"

"At my office. I'll send a car. Don't be late."

He wasn't certain she was fully awake, but he would send her PA to make sure she showed up. It was better this way—he wouldn't give her a chance to talk about returning to Spain.

For now, he'd go along with her crazy baby plan and hope he could convince her there were other things in life than a home and a family. He'd clear his schedule and take some time off. Maybe they could travel. He'd show her Paris and Rome, anywhere she wanted to go.

He'd keep his hands and his mouth to himself from now on. Be her friend. He could do this. All he had to do was stay out of hotel rooms.

She blinked at him sleepily, her long hair rumpled, her mouth sweet. He swayed toward her, longing to kiss those soft pink lips, and had to pull himself up short.

Sitting up, she dragged the thin sheet up over the curves of her breasts, and he stood and headed for the door before he could be tempted to crawl into the bed beside her.

He paused at the door. "And Bella..."

"Yes?"

"Wear a bra."

Chapter Five

"*Wear a bra*," she mimicked under her breath.

Did he think she had no standards? That she needed to be told how to dress in company, no doubt for his posh lawyer? She'd been tempted to ignore the command, but was glad she'd decided against it. Her jeans and shirt were already about as out-of-place as it was possible to get among all the business suits. She could feel eyes tracking her as she followed Sally's brisk march through a huge glass-and-steel reception area.

As if conjured by magic, her "PA" had appeared almost as soon as Rafe left. Maybe Sally had spent the night loitering outside in the corridor in case she was called upon to "assist" with something. This morning, her assignment was to make sure Bella presented herself at Rafe's office, 11:00 a.m., prompt.

"We can't keep him waiting. Mr. Sanchez is a busy man."

Bella was the first to admit that she hadn't been entirely aware of what was going on during her last conversation with Rafe earlier that morning. His broad chest mere inches from her nose, combined with the vivid memory of what it looked like naked, had so dazzled her that she'd failed to focus on the actual words.

Muscles low in her body tightened as she remembered the feel of his hands touching her. Holy crap, that man had clever fingers, and that had only been foreplay. Damn, but she had to stop thinking about sex.

Sex had never been a big deal for her. While she'd enjoyed Gary's lovemaking, it had never made her feel as though she was going to explode out of her skin, burst into flames.

Rafe did. And that made her feel vaguely disloyal to Gary.

Sally had whisked around the hotel suite like a dervish, picking up scraps of underwear, bags, and boxes from the floor, while Bella showered and dressed. Bella considered asking Sally to get her on a plane back to Spain. But while last night hadn't gone entirely as planned, it wasn't all bad. If she'd wanted evidence Rafe did actually want her then she had seen it, in all its naked glory. She resisted the urge to fan herself at the memory.

So she'd go to this meeting, see what he had to say, and could still be on a plane to Spain that afternoon. Or she could stay with her best friend, Amy, while she sorted herself out. Though Amy had only been married a month, and she didn't want to take advantage of her dearest friend.

"So Rafe's company has offices here?" she asked Sally as they waited for the elevator.

"No, the whole building belongs to the company."

"Wow. But it said Santini's above the door."

Sally frowned at her. "Do you actually know anything about Mr. Sanchez?"

Did she? All the stuff Gary had told her tended to be about Rafe rather than his family or his business. Whatever he did, she figured it was high-powered and stressful. He'd always relished the chance to forget about work when he was with them.

Rafe had always been the subject of gossip in the small village where she'd lived. His grandfather might be a shepherd who'd lived in the area all his life, but his mother was an English aristocrat. A wicked woman who seduced the innocent shepherd's son, used him until she was bored, and then sent him home to die of a broken heart. Bella was quite aware the tale had been embellished until it bore little relation to truth.

"His grandfather used to be a shepherd in Spain," she offered.

"He did? Really?" Sally sounded suitably impressed.

"Hmm. I lived out there and worked for his grandfather."

Sally scrunched her brows together. "Looking after sheep?"

"No, he's—" The elevator dinged at that moment, and she was saved any more explanations. Once the doors slid shut, she changed the subject. "So Rafe's company is called Santini's?"

"Yes. Mr. Santini is Mr. Sanchez's stepfather. He—"

"He married Rafe's mother?"

"Obviously. Anyway, he handed the company over to Mr. Sanchez about six years ago."

That would be around the time Bella and Gary married. Rafe had changed at that point, become more serious. His visits brief moments in what she realized now must have been an extremely busy schedule.

"So Rafe runs all this?" she asked.

"He…oh, we're here." Sally cast a quick but all-encompassing glance at Bella and sighed. "Perhaps you could tell him…"

Bella patted her arm. "I'll tell him you tried real hard to get me into something more respectable. And that you're a brilliant PA—by far the best I've ever had."

The elevator doors opened onto another reception area, this one even more luxurious than the one downstairs, but a more understated luxury. Peter North sat behind a desk in front of a set of double doors. It was nice to see a familiar face. He wore a dark business suit and studied Bella with obvious curiosity.

"This is Pete." Sally introduced him to Bella. "Mr. Sanchez's assistant."

"We've already met," Pete said with a grin.

Bella smiled back and waggled her fingers.

"Is he ready for us?" Sally asked.

"Yes. She's to go right in. Alone."

"Oh." Sally seemed slightly deflated. "I'll wait for you here then."

"Rafe said to inform you that you wouldn't be needed for the rest of the day. He'll be taking care of Mrs. Sinclair himself."

"He will?" Sally's glance flickered to Bella, a mixture of envy and commiseration. "I guess I'll see you tomorrow then. Or whenever…give me a call if you need anything."

She nodded, and Sally disappeared into the elevator. Bella nibbled on her lower lip and studied her boots for a minute. When she finally looked up, Pete was watching her, the grin still on his face.

"What?" she asked suspiciously.

"It's just Sally mentioned Rafe's new girlfriend wasn't what she expected. I didn't know it was you."

Bella grimaced. She really didn't need anyone else telling her how glamorous and sophisticated Rafe's *other* girlfriends were. Her gaze wandered to the double doors behind the desk. She should get this over with, but her stomach was fluttering at the thought of facing Rafe after last night.

For God's sake, she'd seen him naked. That had to change

a relationship. Would she ever be able to look him in the face again without seeing his—

The intercom sounded on the desk and interrupted her thoughts. Just as well, really, considering where they'd been heading. Rafe's voice came through tinged with irritation. "Have they arrived yet?"

"Yes, sir."

"Well, why isn't she in here?"

"She's on her way."

Pete raised an eyebrow and gestured to the doors behind him. Bella gave a shrug, straightened her shoulders, and sauntered to the door.

Rafe's office was huge, and three walls were made entirely of glass. She hadn't realized how high up they were, and was drawn to the vast panoramic views of London spread out below them. From here, she could see the Thames meandering through the heart of the city, Tower Bridge, and a glimpse of the London Eye across the water.

"Wow."

She was putting off facing him, and finally she took a deep breath and forced herself to turn around. Two men sat on a long leather sofa, and their eyes pinned on her. Rafe's expression was blank, while the man beside him regarded her with gray eyes as cold as ice.

Ouch.

He must be the lawyer, and from his expression, he no doubt believed she was out to get her claws into Rafe and drain him of every penny she could get her greedy little paws on. She grinned at the thought, and Rafe raised an eyebrow in query.

She waved a hand at the windows. "Nice view."

"It is," Rafe replied smoothly. He rose to his feet and stalked toward her, coming to a halt only inches away. Bella tugged at her ponytail and forced herself to hold her ground.

"You came," he murmured.

It cheered her a little to realize he was in no way 100 percent sure of her. "My PA insisted. Apparently, it was on my agenda."

A smile curled the corner of his lips. He leaned in closer, and before she realized what he meant to do, he kissed her on the cheek. It was quick. The sort of kiss friends would exchange. All the same, her skin tingled, and a little shiver ran through her. She clasped her hands together to stop from reaching for him and dragging his head down so she could kiss him properly—purely to discover if he was as good as she remembered. Instead, she stood like a moron staring into his eyes. Something flickered there, and she had the strangest sensation he was also thinking about kisses and where they could lead.

The lawyer coughed behind her. Rafe stepped back, breaking the eye contact, and she released her breath.

"Are you going to introduce us?"

Bella swung around as the other man spoke for the first time. His voice was smooth and cultured and held as much warmth as his eyes. She glanced at Rafe and quirked a brow.

"Bella, this is John Saunders, my lawyer. John, this is Isabel Sinclair, my…"

"Friend?" she suggested.

"I somehow doubt that, Mrs. Sinclair." The lawyer spoke in that cool, clipped voice.

"You do?"

"Bella *is* a friend," Rafe snapped. "And I'd appreciate it if you kept that in mind." He sounded pissed, but his lawyer appeared unfazed. A brave man. She glanced back at Rafe. He shrugged. "John has drawn up the papers. They're ready for you to sign."

"I don't want to sign anything."

"Of course you do, Mrs. Sinclair. The terms are extremely

generous."

The man was starting to seriously irritate her. He was probably hoping he would annoy her so much that she'd turn around and walk out. Well, she was made of sterner stuff, and he wouldn't drive her away. She hated lawyers, especially pompous, superior ones, and wouldn't give this arrogant man the satisfaction. She stuck out her hand. "Give me the papers."

He studied her, his expression still cold, but a flicker of uncertainty showed in his eyes as though she wasn't quite what he expected.

Hey, someone else who thought she wasn't like Rafe's usual girlfriends. What a surprise.

Rafe strolled across to the desk, picked up a folder, and handed it to her. It was thick.

She frowned. "All this for me?"

He nodded. "I still think we need time to get to know each other better. This is just in case we…decide to go ahead."

She suspected he'd been about to say something else. Hopefully, along the lines of—*in case we can't keep our hands off each other.*

"I have to read all this?" She flipped through the pages. There must have been at least twenty, all covered in small type.

"I would suggest you read it carefully," John Saunders replied. "We wouldn't want you to come back later and say you didn't understand."

She pursed her lips. "If I don't, I won't be signing anything. But I'm sure you can redo it in words someone like me can comprehend."

Rafe's lips twitched at her retort. "John will stick around in case you have any questions."

"Lovely," she murmured. She wandered across to the sofa and sank into the corner. Reaching down, she unlaced her boots, kicked them off, and sat cross-legged. This was going to take time, and she might as well be comfortable.

As she opened the file and started reading, the skin prickled along the back of her neck. Glancing up, she found both men regarding her intensely and she scowled.

"Are you two going to stare at me the whole time I read this? Because it's making me just a little bit uncomfortable."

Rafe nodded to the lawyer and gestured to the seat by the desk. "Get on with some work if you want to."

John took the chair but sat staring into space, a slightly puzzled frown on his face. That just left Rafe. Bella glared at him and raised an eyebrow. He ignored the hint, sank down onto the opposite corner of the sofa, and sat with his arms behind his head, long legs stretched out in front of him.

"You know, I'm sure someone mentioned you were a busy man. Don't you have something important to do?" she asked.

"Nothing that won't wait."

"What about getting me some coffee?" she asked hopefully. Her brain didn't function properly with him so close. But he only leaned across and pressed a button on the desk. "Pete, could you sort us out some coffee?"

She glowered, but it was probably the best she was going to get, and she shut him out as well as she could and went back to her reading. She hardly noticed when someone placed a tray of coffee next to her. But she picked up the cup and drank absently.

Despite what she'd said, she'd been worried she'd need a lawyer of her own to understand this. But the document was written in plain English rather than lawyer gobbledygook. The contract didn't in any way impose on her the need to sleep with Rafe. It just set out what would happen if they did and subsequently had a child together.

The document explained the settlement in detail. And

the terms were very generous. Too generous.

"This allowance…" she said, glancing up.

"It's as much as you're going to get and twice as much as the number I recommended," John shot back instantly.

She curled her lip at him and resisted the urge to stick out her tongue. "I was going to say it's too much."

"It's good," Rafe replied. "I don't want a child of mine wanting for anything."

She was slowly becoming aware how wealthy Rafe was. It made her twitchy—she really did want to stand on her own two feet, provide for her child. She pushed the worries aside and waved the document in the air. "Is this actually legally binding?"

"As legally binding as we can make it," John said. "This isn't exactly a common occurrence, and it's the first I've drawn up of its kind. But at the least you'd have to fight it in court if you decide you want more later."

"I don't want more. In fact I don't want any."

"That's not an option," Rafe said. "And this is a deal breaker. You have my baby, then I will provide for it."

She nibbled on her lower lip as she attempted to think logically. The money made her uncomfortable, but she could always invest it for her child. The truth was, she was going to sign. It meant nothing to her, but if signing eased Rafe's concerns, then why not? She peeped over the top of the paper and found him observing her, his blue eyes gleaming through half-lowered lashes. He caught her gaze and a slow smile curved his lips. Heat pooled low in her belly, her breasts tingled, and she looked away quickly and swallowed.

Friends!

He didn't look at her as though he wanted to be her friend.

She swallowed. "I really don't want your money."

"I know."

That was something at least. Taking a deep breath, she stood, crossed to the desk, and slammed the document down. "Give me a pen."

Rafe's expression was carefully blank, and she realized again that he was in no way sure of her. Her heart pounded as she signed and dated the document, and then the copy John placed in front of her. She watched as Rafe signed as well.

John picked up the papers and examined them, then placed one copy in his briefcase and slid the second back to her. "This is yours. I suggest you keep it somewhere safe. Preferably give it to your lawyer."

"I don't have a lawyer," she replied sweetly. "I think they're all money-grubbing parasites."

She was almost sure a smile flickered across his face, but it was gone before she could be sure. He held out his hand and she grasped it automatically.

"Good luck, Mrs. Sinclair. I think you're going to need it."

She frowned as he released her hand and then walked away, Rafe at his side. Bella turned to stare out of the window. This time she didn't even see the view below her.

· · ·

Rafe hustled John out of the room before Bella could change her mind.

She'd signed. She was his.

He started at the thought. In no way was Bella his. She could never be his. And that contract meant less than nothing. But at least she wasn't going to disappear in the immediate future. Or hunt for some other man to act as sperm donor.

He couldn't ever remember a business deal that had caused him so much anxiety. Sweat broke out on his forehead when she'd glared at him over the papers.

John paused at the door, and Rafe shifted impatiently wanting the other man gone.

"Maybe this will go all right," John murmured. "She's certainly not what I expected. In fact, I'm almost tempted to think she's the one I should worry about. Does she understand what she's getting into?"

"I've known her seven years. She's twenty-four and a widow—I think she can look after herself."

"Maybe. Anyway, I hope neither of you ends up regretting this."

Rafe glanced back at Bella. She stood sideways to them, hands stuffed into the back pockets of her jeans as she gazed out the windows. The faded denim clung to the long, slender length of her legs, molded to her bottom. His body tightened at the sight. He tried to ignore the sensation. If Bella came out of this unscathed and found a way to move on—which she would if he could keep his dick in his pants—then he'd be content. If not happy. "I won't regret it."

John shook his head and left the office. Rafe began to close the door behind him, but in the end decided to leave it open.

He'd almost given in last night. Bella had the ability to make him forget all his good intentions, and he suspected that if he ever did cave and make love to her, he'd find it next to impossible to let her go. He couldn't do that to her. He couldn't tie her to a relationship that would be counter to everything she wanted in life. She'd come to hate him in the end.

This way was better. They could be friends—all he had to do was make sure he wasn't alone with her. Shouldn't be too hard. By the time the three months was done, she'd be over this baby business. All he had to do was show her how exciting her life could be.

As he approached, she turned to face him. "Does it

bother you that your friend thinks I'm a money-grubbing man-eater?"

"No." He crossed the room and sank onto the sofa, pulled off his tie, and opened the top button of his shirt. He stifled a yawn. He'd been tense, on edge, in no way sure how this would go. Now he could relax.

He'd thought he'd known Bella well, but he was seeing a new side to her. She'd given John as good as she got. And John had liked her for it despite his obvious better judgment. "John's just wary. He doesn't know you. And he has my best interests at heart."

"Well, that's what friends are for. So what now? Am I in the way? I can take myself off if you need to get back to work."

"No, I've had Pete cancel my appointments for the rest of the day."

"You have?" She cocked her head to one side and studied him. "We could go back to the hotel and have some lunch. I'm starving."

His mind immediately conjured up an image of the big four-poster bed. Lobster and champagne. Bella naked…

"No, I'll take you out for lunch," he said.

Shit. He was crap at this friend thing.

Chapter Six

Rafe had that slightly panicked look again.

What did he think she was suggesting? Room service in bed? And even if she was, which she wasn't, why should the idea send him into a tizzy? All he had to do was say no.

"I'm really not dressed for eating out." She kept her tone casual and waved a hand over her jeans and T-shirt. "The hotel would be better." She considered him for a moment. That little telltale tic was jumping in his cheek again. And something occurred to her. He really was serious about the friendship thing, but he was finding it hard to stick to. Some perverse little devil made her tease him just to see his reaction. "We could get room service."

He pressed a finger to his forehead, and she held her breath. Yes or no? "I don't think so," he said, and she exhaled loudly.

This whole setup was doing her head in. Now she was flirting with Rafe. That hadn't been part of the deal. But it was his fault. All this hot-cold-hot was messing with her. She'd never considered she would actually get pleasure from the deal, that she would actually want Rafe that way, but last night had proved how delusional that was. Part of her wished she could remain detached, because it felt like she was crossing a line, but she couldn't deny the underlying excitement.

"No," he continued, "a restaurant to celebrate our agreement. So what would you like?"

Well, if she wasn't going to get Rafe served up on a plate, she knew exactly what she wanted. "Pizza."

"Pizza?" He sounded as though he'd never heard of it. Then he nodded. "Pizza—why not?"

Rafe rose slowly to his feet, stretched like a lazy jungle animal, then ran his gaze down the length of her and smiled. "But perhaps you should put some shoes on first, *querida*. And don't forget your contract."

That was another thing—if he was determined that they remain friends for the foreseeable future, perhaps she should tell him to stop calling her *querida* in that hot, sexy voice. It did weird things to her insides.

The outer office was empty, but as they crossed the room, the elevator doors opened and a woman stepped out. Rafe tensed and came to a halt. He swore in Spanish under his breath. So not totally happy to see whoever it was. Bella regarded the woman curiously.

Glamorous and sophisticated—no doubt this was a prime example of Rafe's "usual" women. An old flame? Or a current one, and Rafe was upset because he didn't want their paths to cross? She hadn't thought to check whether he was in a relationship—but surely he would have told her.

The woman was tall, with striking bone structure, blond hair swept up in an elegant chignon, dark blue eyes, and perfect makeup. She was dressed in a charcoal-gray suit that made her look both businesslike and sexy at the same time. It also gave her the appearance of maturity, but when Bella studied her more closely she realized the woman couldn't be more than nineteen or twenty.

Cradle-snatcher! Bella gave a sideways peek at Rafe. Whoever this girl was, he didn't look pleased to see her.

"Gina," he muttered. "What the hell are you doing here?"

The woman cast Bella a curious glance, ignored Rafe's question, strolled over, and kissed him on the cheek. "Aren't you pleased to see me?"

"No."

"But Rafael, you told me you would take me more seriously if I acted more seriously." She gestured down at her business suit. "Don't you think I look the part?"

"The part of what, exactly? What do you want, Gina?"

"A job, of course." She glanced from Rafe to Bella as if suddenly realizing he wasn't alone and raised an eyebrow, her expression cooling visibly. "Who's this?"

She might as well have said *what's this*, from the disdain in her tone. When Rafe didn't answer immediately, Bella glanced at him. For the first time ever, he appeared discomforted.

She almost felt sorry for him. Almost. Not quite. Okay, she admitted to herself—not at all.

The look the girl was giving her was far from complimentary, as though Bella were something the cat had dragged in, chewed up, and then spat out again. If she'd been more sensitive it might have hurt. Even so, a small part wished she had just a little of this young woman's poise. Next to these two glamorous people she felt less than adequate, and she hated that.

She shouldn't give a damn what Rafe's other, hopefully-ex-girlfriend thought of her.

But she did care, and the realization stirred her temper. Bella inched a step closer to him, rested her fingers on his arm, and smiled sweetly.

"Hi there, I'm Bella, I'm Rafe's..." She shrugged as the correct term eluded her, then glanced at the contract she still held in her hand. "We're going to have a baby together."

As soon as the words were out, she couldn't believe she'd said them.

Two sets of dark blue eyes gazed at her in disbelief, and then a torrent of Italian burst from the girl. Rafe replied in equally irate Italian, and for a minute the two were engrossed in each other. Bella peeked at the door and wondered whether she could sneak out without them noticing. Rafe turned briefly her way and cast her a narrow-eyed glance that said, *don't you dare.* Just to make sure, he grabbed her hand and held on to it as the argument continued. Bella wished she understood, but while she spoke a few words of Italian, this was way too fast.

"Shut up, Gina." Rafe raised his other hand and made a cutting movement. He turned to Bella, and his fingers tightened on hers almost painfully. "Bella, allow me to introduce you to my sister, Giovanna Santini."

His sister?

Oh Lord, what had she done? She'd forgotten he even had a sister.

She licked her dry lips and gave a casual shrug. "Um, er... hello. That last thing I said...I didn't mean...I don't suppose you would consider...forgetting it?"

"Don't say any more, *querida.*" Rafe's tone was gentle, but she could hear the frustration beneath the softly spoken words. He turned back to his sister. "Gina, this is Isabel Sinclair, a friend of mine. And no, she is not carrying my baby."

Some devil of mischief had the word "yet" hovering on the tip of Bella's tongue. Thankfully, she managed to swallow it.

"But—" Gina began. Rafe gave her a look that would

have cut Bella off in midflow, and Gina clamped her lips closed.

"*Madre de dios*. Go, I'll talk to you later," Rafe ordered.

Suddenly, Gina looked very young. She turned and stomped toward the elevator. But as she waited for the doors to open, her shoulders stiffened and she whirled around, her eyes narrowing. "Just wait until I tell Mother about this."

As a parting line, it was brilliant. Rafe didn't seem quite so impressed. He pressed his fingers to his eyes as the doors slid shut behind her.

"Your sister seems nice."

Rafe gave her a long look, and she squirmed.

"Okay, I'm sorry." Bella kept her voice meek though it was a struggle; she'd never been good at apologizing for her misbehavior, even when she knew she was in the wrong. "I thought she was your girlfriend."

"Why the hell would you think that?"

"Because she's gorgeous and glamorous and apparently that's what all your girlfriends are like. Except me." She stared at the polished floor for a second, then back at Rafe. "Will she tell anyone?"

"Everyone, I would think. She'll probably put an announcement in the *Times* as well."

"Have I caused you a lot of trouble?"

"Endless." He ran a hand through his hair, and suddenly the hard lines of his handsome face relaxed, and he chuckled. "It was almost worth it for the look on Gina's face. *Dios*."

Bella sighed. "I don't normally blurt things out like that. I guess you must be a bad influence."

"I hope so. One thing…?"

She looked up at his silkily spoken words and glanced at him warily. "Yes?"

"Why would you tell my girlfriend that we were having a baby?" He studied her closely. "Were you jealous, *querida*?"

"In your dreams."

Jealous? Surely not. But a cold, hard lump congealed in her middle.

He still had hold of her hand. Now he tugged her toward the elevator where his sister had disappeared only minutes earlier. After pressing the button, he leaned one shoulder against the wall as he surveyed her. She tried to keep her attention on the vee of golden skin at his throat, but couldn't resist a peek at his face. His earlier irritation seemed to have vanished completely, to be replaced by a look of sleepy satisfaction that sent a ripple of anticipation running through her. She had the distinct idea that he didn't believe she wasn't jealous. Followed by the notion that her jealousy wasn't entirely repugnant to him. Talk about mixed signals.

He smiled. "And now—*I'm* getting hungry."

Bella was starving. But she wasn't sure pizza was going to fix that.

He took her to a small Italian bistro. She suspected it was more expensive than it appeared; the other diners all looked well-bred and well-dressed with that air only serious money conveys. But it was quaint, with low wooden beams and checked tablecloths, the air redolent with the scent of herbs and fresh bread.

The hostess didn't blink an eye at Bella's jeans, just led them to a small corner table with a single red rose in a crystal vase.

"What can I get you to drink?" she asked.

Rafe answered. "Champagne—Bollinger 2002."

Bella waited until the woman had disappeared. "I take it that's a good year. But I've got to warn you, it will be wasted on me—I'm used to my own stuff." The farm had a small vineyard, and they'd always made their own wine.

"You'll enjoy it, I promise."

They both ordered pizza, and Bella relaxed as the waiter expertly opened the wine. She sipped the pale liquid, feeling the bubbles all the way down in her stomach. "I really am sorry about what I said to your sister. Even if she had been your girlfriend, I shouldn't have told her that."

"No, you shouldn't," he agreed. "But it's done. Let's forget it until we get the fallout."

She was happy to, but couldn't totally dismiss her guilt. "Usually, I'm quite happy with how I am, but she made me feel..."

He quirked a brow and she forced herself to continue.

"...inadequate, scruffy...a mess."

He ran his gaze over her, making her squirm in the seat. She picked up her glass and took a healthy slug, and nearly choked.

"You're beautiful," he said, taking a sip of his wine and continuing to study her over the rim of his glass. "But I'm sure a lot of people must have told you that."

Aw, he thought she was beautiful. Her stomach fluttered, and warmth stole over her. "Only Gary. And he was biased."

"He had good taste."

"Maybe. As I said, normally it doesn't bother me but you're always so—" She broke off again and considered him for a minute. He was so smooth, so groomed, not a hair out of place. She could never stay that tidy for more than five minutes at a time. "Do you mind if I do something?"

A wary expression crept into his eyes. "What?"

• • •

Rafe held his breath as she put down her glass. He never knew what Bella would do. She reached across the table and raked her hand through his hair. The stroke of her fingers against his scalp sent prickles of awareness shooting down his spine to settle in his dick. He swallowed but didn't move. At least his reaction was hidden beneath the table.

It felt good to relax his guard. After all, what could happen in here? He could hardly lose control and take her on the table amid the other diners.

Now she was sitting back, a satisfied smirk on her face.

He cleared his throat. "What was that for?"

"I just wanted to make you a little less perfect."

Shock hit him at her words. Was that how she saw him? "I'm far from perfect."

"Come on, Rafe, you always look impeccable."

He considered her words and the irony that she should see him as perfect, when in fact he was fundamentally flawed. People only ever saw what was on the surface.

These days, he rarely thought about how he looked or what he wore. "My mother was something of a perfectionist. I suppose I wanted to please her, and it saved being nagged if I got it right first time. Now it's just become a habit."

"Really? My dad was the same." She grinned. "It didn't stick with me. Though I suspect I maybe went the other way just to annoy him."

"He was in the army, wasn't he?"

"Yes, a sergeant. Gary's father was his commanding officer. That's how I met Gary. My mum and dad divorced when I wasn't much more than a baby. But Mum died when I was eight, and I went back to live with my dad."

"I'm sorry."

She'd lost everyone. Mother, father, husband, and baby. Was it so strange that she wanted this baby? Someone of her own. Guilt prodded him in the gut. Maybe he was wrong to lie to her, however much he'd convinced himself it was for her own good. He also suspected there was a whole load of self-deception going on inside his head. But he didn't want to think about that, and he wasn't ready to let her go. Would he ever be?

The food arrived then, and they were silent for a few minutes. Bella ate her pizza with gusto, as she did everything. He watched with fascination as she licked tomato sauce from her fingers.

"Have you spoken with your grandfather recently?" she asked.

He let out a sigh of relief—a safe subject. "Yes. He's good—much better. He's a tough old man. I wish I could persuade him to move to London, but he loves his home."

"And you hate it. Why? I've always wondered."

He sipped his wine while he thought about his answer. "I always blamed the place for taking my father away from us. One of the things I remember most about him was wanting us all to return to Spain. My mother wouldn't consider it. She loved city life. In the end, I guess he loved the place more than he loved us."

"I don't believe that. There must have been something else going on."

She was so perceptive, but she was also venturing onto dangerous ground. "It turned out there were other reasons, but I didn't know that at the time."

She opened her mouth, no doubt to ask what the other reasons were, and he cut her off.

"Back then, the place was very different. This was before I had the villa built. Grandfather lived in a cottage, no water, no electricity"—he gave a visible shudder—"no telephone."

She laughed. "It can't have been that bad."

"After living in London and New York, it was like being plunged into the Middle Ages. It was hell. If I was ever bad as a child, my mother would threaten to send me to live out there. Gary was the only one who made those visits bearable.

He loved the mountains—turned the whole thing into an adventure."

"Yeah, he was full of the place whenever he got back. I was always so jealous."

"London is better. I'll show you London. And Paris and Rome."

"You will? I thought you were 'a busy man.'"

"Well, I think I can take a couple of days off. In the last few years the only days I've had free were when I visited Spain."

"Why? You're the boss—surely you could delegate?"

"Not so much. I took over the company when my stepfather became ill. It was a tough time. My mother doesn't take illness very well—so I wanted things to go smoothly. Also a lot of people felt I was too young—so I had something to prove."

"Sally said you did a fantastic job."

Rafe waved away the comment, but a smile tugged at his lips. "We've come through it okay."

"Always so modest. So we have the weekend. I'd love to go on the Eye. And ride on a double-decker bus, and go to the zoo. The rest is up to you." She started on a second piece of pizza.

"How are you for money?" he asked. "If you need any, you'll let me know?"

"Money?"

She sounded as though she didn't know what the stuff was. "I should have mentioned it earlier. It never occurred to me—I presumed Gary would have left you better off."

"Gary didn't have any money. He was due to come into a trust fund when he was thirty, but he died before that." She tilted her head and considered him for a few seconds. "Anyway, I don't want your money."

"Why?"

"Taking money from you would be weird." Her brows drew together as she thought about her answer. "I'm still trying to reconcile myself to accepting your money if I have your baby. But if I took it now, I'd be like your mistress but without the sex part."

She took another bite of pizza. This time her tongue swiped tomato sauce from her lower lip. He wished she hadn't mentioned sex. But now that she had, he couldn't leave it alone. "You want sex?" He was pleased his voice sounded normal.

She shrugged, the movement raising her breasts beneath her T-shirt. At least she was wearing a bra, though he could still make out her nipples beneath the thin material.

"I hadn't really thought about it except as a means to an end. But I guess so. I'm a normal woman, after all, and you're…."

"I'm?"

"Well, I suppose you're good-looking and you've been around."

"I think I've just been insulted."

She grinned. "I didn't mean to, but you're my friend. I never thought about you like that. And then you kissed me and suddenly…" She shrugged, and he held his breath. "And suddenly I did."

And his dick just got a whole lot harder.

"But don't worry about it," she continued. "It's not your problem." She pursed her lips. "Hey, maybe I'll get a vibrator."

He'd been about to swallow. Now he spurted champagne across the table. "Sorry," he muttered as his mind flooded with a deluge of totally inappropriate images. She obviously had no clue of the effect she had on him. He wondered if anyone would notice if he poured the rest of the champagne in his lap.

Maybe he'd buy her a vibrator. Then he could fantasize…

Damn, he was one sick bastard.

"Aren't you hungry?" she asked.

Her pizza was finished. He'd barely touched his. He wasn't hungry, at least not for food. "Help yourself," he said.

She picked up another slice. "I suppose if we decide to go ahead with this baby, then we'll have to have sex. You're just going to have to close your eyes and think of England."

He cleared his throat. "Actually, I was thinking more along the lines of artificial insemination."

The half-eaten slice of pizza dropped from her fingers.

Chapter Seven

Artificial insemination?

In the two days since he'd uttered those terrible words, they had never been far from the forefront of Bella's mind. Now, as she paced the hotel room while she waited for Rafe, they repeated themselves over and over in her head.

Yesterday, they had spent the whole day together. They'd visited London Zoo. It had been fun, and for a while they'd come close to the relaxed relationship they'd shared while Gary was alive. Apparently, Rafe had never been to a zoo— and she'd thought *her* childhood had been deprived. He'd teased her, and laughed with her, and treated her like his kid sister. Actually, from what she had seen of his interaction with Gina, he treated her better than his kid sister. But he didn't touch her. Afterward, he'd taken her to dinner in a crowded restaurant, kept the conversational subjects strictly impersonal—he was so good at that—and then left her at her hotel room door with a totally asexual peck on the cheek.

She'd fallen asleep with the words "artificial insemination" reverberating in her mind, souring her mood.

It went against the whole substance of their agreement. He was supposed to get the pleasure of sex with a woman he desired, namely herself, and she got the baby she dreamed about. Though she was beginning to realize that the pleasure would not be one-sided. Rafe was obviously really good at the sex thing. She wanted him, and she'd been so sure he wanted her. Now it appeared she had been deluded after all. What the hell was wrong with her?

She was hurt and confused and then hurt again.

Today, despite being Sunday, he'd had to go into work in the morning, but this afternoon, he was going to take her on a tour of the city. He'd suggested the limousine and driver. She quashed that idea and requested an open-topped double-decker bus. But first she was going to insist he talk to her, get everything out in the open. When he came up to collect her, she would invite him in politely, then lock the door and sit on him until he explained to her the convoluted workings of his brain. She felt marginally better once she had a plan.

The hotel phone rang and she picked it up.

"I'm down in reception," Rafe said.

A frown tugged at her brows. "Aren't you coming up?"

"No." And he ended the call. Just like that.

For a moment, she glared at the phone in her hand. So much for her plan, thwarted at the first hurdle. She ground her teeth together, then slammed the phone down, grabbed her bag, and headed for the door.

It occurred to her as the elevator glided down that for the last two years, since Gary's death, she'd been numb. Now at last she was awake. Like a prince in a fairy tale, Rafe had kissed her and woken her up—in mind and body. Something else occurred to her—maybe it wasn't Rafe in particular; maybe he had just been around at the right time, and she'd respond in the same way to any good-looking guy.

Holy shit. She was a cliché. A sex-starved widow,

desperate for a man. Rafe was right to be afraid. If this was a fairy tale, she wasn't the princess, she was the wicked witch or the evil stepmother.

Maybe I should kiss some other men while I'm here. See what happens.

Then the door slid open and there he was. *Crap.* Her heartbeat stuttered and then began to race. Even in black jeans and a white linen shirt, he appeared glamorous and gorgeous, his expression hidden behind dark aviator glasses.

She gave a dramatic sigh.

Her prince.

• • •

She was alone in the lift when the door opened, and for a few seconds she didn't move, just stood staring at him, and then she sighed, loudly.

"What?" he asked.

She took the few steps toward him. "I was just thinking, coming down in the elevator, that you're like a fairy-tale prince."

He snorted and then studied her for a moment. "Have you been drinking?"

"Of course not. But don't worry. I decided it was maybe just a proximity thing. I haven't exactly come into contact with many potential princes. I probably just need to get out more."

He didn't like the sound of that, though hadn't it been the original plan? Get her back here, show her that life could be fun and her dreams were still within her grasp. That maybe her fairy-tale prince was waiting around the corner. But it wasn't him.

She was dressed in jeans and a black lace-trimmed tank top, her hair in a ponytail, her face free of makeup. She looked beautiful, and he had to fight the urge to push her back into the elevator and kiss her senseless. That wasn't going to happen.

She was watching him speculatively, lips pursed.

He was quite aware she was still pissed at him for the artificial insemination comment. That she'd been itching to talk about it yesterday, but he hadn't been ready to talk. He had no clue what to say.

It had been another of those little trips into crazy land. With hindsight, he could see that the suggestion had been some subconscious, totally mad idea that if they went the artificial insemination route, then he could pretend the donor sperm was his, and tie her to him with this baby she wanted so desperately. It had only taken seconds for him to realize the insanity of the idea. But he hadn't been able to take the words back. He was seriously losing it.

"Let's go," he said. The car was parked in front of the hotel, and the doorman hurried across and opened the back door for them.

Bella came to a halt short of the car. "We can walk to the pickup point," she said, pulling a map out of her bag and waving it under his nose. "It's only around the corner."

Ten minutes later, he was admiring the sway of her ass as she climbed the stairs to the second level of the bus, then led him down the narrow space between the seats. She grinned as she plonked herself down on the backseat and patted the cushion beside her. "Best seats on the bus," she said with such obvious glee that he couldn't help but smile.

"I don't think I've ever been on a bus," he murmured, taking the seat beside her.

"I'm so glad I'm extending your horizons, Mr. Sanchez."

The bus filled up quickly, and soon they were driving slowly through the streets of London. Bella had the earphones in, listening as the tour guide told her about London, but he was content to relax and watch her. After half an hour she turned around and looked behind them, then frowned and removed the earphones.

"Tell me that's not your car following us," she muttered, peering over her shoulder at the road behind them. He followed her gaze; the limo was clearly visible behind a black cab.

He shrugged. "I wanted to be prepared. I thought you might get bored and want to get off."

"Hoped I might get bored, you mean." She studied him for a second. "Are you bored?"

"No." And it was the truth.

He waited for her to put the earphones back on. Instead, she studied him, a calculating expression flashing in her eyes, and his muscles tightened in anticipation.

"So," she said, "I'm wearing some of the clothes you bought me."

"You are." He looked her over, but was pretty sure neither the jeans nor the top were new.

"Hmm." She licked her lips as she watched him, and heat coiled in his stomach. Lowering her voice, she added, "The black lace bra with red ribbons."

He couldn't help it—his gaze dropped to her breasts. Was it his imagination, or did she thrust them out just a little bit?

She inched nearer on the seat, so her thigh touched his, and leaned in close to whisper, "And the matching thong. Though I've got to say, it's not the most comfortable thing I've ever worn." She wriggled a little on the seat, and his dick jerked in his pants. He had a strange idea that this was some devious payback for the artificial insemination comment. And for his refusal to talk about the artificial insemination comment. But he wasn't going to rise. A double-decker bus was not the place.

"Stop it, *querida*."

"Stop what?" she asked, all wide-eyed innocence.

"You know what." Reaching across, he picked up her earphones and placed them gently on her head.

She scowled, but turned her attention to the sights of London. He sat staring straight ahead, legs crossed to hide his growing erection, doing his best to banish the image of Bella in nothing but a black lace thong from his mind. And once again failing miserably. He had finally gotten himself under control when she turned to him and grabbed his arm. "Look, there's Buckingham Palace. Can we get off?"

"Do we have to get on again?" But he was only teasing. He was enjoying himself. At least when he wasn't suffering the extreme discomfort and potential embarrassment of an erection on public transport.

She eyed him up. "We can go somewhere and talk instead."

"We'll get back on."

• • •

Bella put her hand over her mouth to cover the yawn. They'd stopped off at Buckingham Palace, Saint Paul's Cathedral, and the Tower of London. Her feet ached, and her head was stuffed full of history. Now they were in a private capsule on the London Eye, slowly rising as the huge wheel rotated, carrying them up above the city.

She'd had a wonderful day. At least once she'd finally given up on getting him to talk or kiss her. After that she'd had fun. He made a good friend. She cast him a sideways glance. He stood at the front of the capsule, hands in his pockets, staring out.

"Have you ever been here before?" she asked.

He turned to her. "No."

"You grew up in London and you've never been to the

zoo, or the tower, or Saint Paul's?"

"My mother wasn't really into sightseeing. But I only lived here until I was ten. Then we moved between Rome and New York."

His life was just so different from hers. From anyone's, she guessed.

"I've enjoyed myself," he said.

"Don't sound so surprised," she countered.

For a few minutes they stood side by side in silence. The sun was going down, the lights coming on across the city, reflecting off the dark water of the River Thames far below them. It was a magical sight. Without thought she turned to him, took a step closer, and wrapped her arms around his waist. She sensed his hesitation, then his arms enveloped her and he pulled her tight against him. Beneath her cheek, his heart beat steadily, and his warm breath ruffled her hair. For the first time since he'd uttered those awful words, she felt at peace. He shifted back slightly, and his hands cupped her cheeks.

She raised her face to him as the door at the rear of the capsule opened and the hostess stepped in, wheeling a trolley with glasses and a bottle of champagne.

Damn. Damn. Damn.

Rafe stepped back, his hands dropping to his sides.

"Are you ready for dinner, sir, madam?"

Grrr. No.

She wanted Rafe to kiss her. Had he arranged this, so even up here they wouldn't be alone? Then her stomach rumbled. She was starving, and she exhaled loudly.

"Bring it on," she muttered.

Rafe rested a hand on her back as he steered her to the table and waited until she was seated, then took the chair opposite.

She scowled and narrowed her eyes. "Saved by dinner."

He gave her a rueful smile. "Have some champagne."

So she did. Then inhaled deeply. How could she stay mad in such beautiful surroundings? He'd arranged all this for her. "So, tell me about the first time you met Gary."

He raised a brow as if she'd surprised him. "It wasn't very exciting. He was a baby, an ugly little thing. I was four."

"Tell me anyway."

By the time Rafe dropped her back at the hotel, she was too tired and fuzzy to make a fuss when he dropped an entirely too chaste kiss on her forehead and stepped back.

"I'll pick you up tomorrow night," he said.

"Can't. I'm seeing Amy."

For a second she thought he might argue, then he gave a curt nod. "Tuesday, then. Sleep well."

And once again he was gone.

She closed the hotel room door behind her and sank down on the sofa. It had been bittersweet talking about Gary, but in some ways the conversation had cleansed her. Rafe was the one person who had known her husband as well as she did. Had loved him as much.

She recognized that on some deep level, she had felt guilty about this thing with Rafe. As though she still owed her loyalty to Gary. Tonight had made her remember him more clearly. Above anything else, he would have wanted her to be happy.

She stared down at the gold wedding band she still wore and blinked away a tear. Then she slipped the ring from her finger.

Chapter Eight

"Okay, I'll give you the benefit of my expertise," Amy said. "But first you've got to explain where you're going with this. Because I think there's something you're not telling me."

Bella took a sip of her wine. "Going?" she asked as innocently as she could manage.

"Come on, Isabel, you ask me for advice on how to seduce a guy and you expect me not to want details."

"Not expect—no. More of a hope, really."

"Never going to happen."

They were in Amy's bedroom at her house in Notting Hill. Bella had actually come over to borrow some clothes. She was going to try to get a temporary job tomorrow and needed to look smart. Or at least smarter than she did right now. There was certainly nothing suitable for an interview among the stuff Rafe had bought for her—it was all silk and lace.

They'd gone through Amy's wardrobe and picked out a couple of business suits. They fit perfectly. They'd added a couple of silky tank tops to the pile and a pair of three-inch heels. They'd always been able to interchange clothes.

Afterward, Bella had pulled her jeans and T-shirt back on, while Amy opened a bottle and insisted on hearing the details of everything Bella had been up to. It occurred to her, somewhere after they'd finished the first bottle, that maybe she could get some constructive advice while she was here.

"So come on," Amy said. "Spill the beans. Just who exactly are you planning to seduce? Tell me everything."

Amy was an investigative journalist and the nosiest person Bella had ever met. And she loved her like a sister. They'd met at boarding school when they were both thirteen. Amy had just been expelled from the swankiest girls' school in England for writing an exposé on the sex lives of teachers. She'd ended up at the less-than-swanky institute where Bella spent her school days. They'd become immediate friends.

The problem was, she was pretty sure Amy would consider her current situation beyond crazy. She squirmed as she worked out the best way to phrase her words.

"Hmm, you don't want to tell me," Amy said. "Now, why is that, I wonder?" She took a sip of her wine and regarded Bella over the glass. "Spill."

Bella took a deep breath and blurted. "I'm here with Rafe."

Amy put down her glass and sank onto the bed. "Rafe? As in Rafael Sanchez?"

"The one and only."

"And when you say you're here with Rafe, what does that involve? Are you and he…?" She waggled her eyebrows in a suggestive manner. "Though wait a minute, if you're asking me for seduction advice, I'm guessing no."

Bella nodded glumly. "You'd be guessing right."

"But you want to. I thought you were just friends."

"We were. We are."

"You don't seem too sure."

Bella refilled her glass with red wine, handed the bottle to Amy, and leaned back against the headboard. "I asked him…" She ran a hand through her hair, took a deep breath. "It all started because he kissed me. Before that, I never thought he'd ever seen me as a woman, but he wanted me, really wanted me. Or so I thought."

"And you want him."

"Not at first. He was just a means to an end."

"What end?"

"A baby. I wanted a baby."

"Oh, sweetie." Amy reached across and gave her a quick hug. "One day you'll find someone else."

"I don't want another husband. But I do want a family. And Rafe seemed perfect, and he wanted me, so it would be a fair exchange. So I asked him and he—"

"You asked Rafael Sanchez for a baby?"

"Hmm. At first he was shocked, then he said he would, but only after we'd spent some time together and I was sure it was what I wanted. And I thought we'd be…you know."

"Shagging like rabbits?"

"Yes. But there's been nothing." *Well, nothing much apart from that one hot make-out session at the hotel,* but she didn't want to get into that.

"Except the kiss."

"It was an amazing kiss."

"It must have been." Amy sounded skeptical. "So now you want to seduce him?"

"We signed this contract, mainly about what happens if I have Rafe's baby, and I thought we were there. Then over lunch afterward he said…" She gritted her teeth. She still couldn't get her head around it. "He said…*artificial insemination.*"

Amy choked on her wine and then cleared her throat. "And what did you say?"

"I was cool. Well, okay, I lost it for a minute, but then I was cool, or at least coolish."

Amy chuckled.

"But really—the only way I felt I could ask him for the baby was because I thought he wanted me. And now it seems he doesn't, that he can't bear to even touch me. How can I have his baby—and take his money—which he totally insists on—if he gets nothing in return?"

"Maybe he doesn't feel right using you for sex."

Bella scowled. "Jesus. If anyone is using anyone, it's me using him. And anyway, it's different now. He wouldn't be using me, because I want him. Really want him."

"Did you tell him that?"

"He refuses to discuss it. All he said was we would talk about it when I was sure the baby was what I wanted."

"That's very civilized. And you've been together since?"

"Yeah."

"And?"

"And nothing. We're friends. We did 'friends stuff.'" Bella sighed. "In some ways it was great. We had fun, talked about Gary. He misses him."

Amy patted her knee, and the gesture nearly brought tears to Bella's eyes. She took a deep breath and continued. "And at the end of the day, he drops me off at the hotel and kisses me chastely on the forehead."

"Maybe he's realized he can't see past the whole married-to-my-best-friend scenario."

"Don't think it hasn't occurred to me." Bella forced herself to think about it for the umpteenth time and finally shook her head. "No. He does want me. Sometimes he gets this look in his eyes. And that kiss..." Not to mention that amazingly impressive erection. She swallowed the last of her wine and held out her glass for more, then noticed the bottle was empty.

"But you did say they were like brothers. Maybe he thinks it would be some weird sort of incest."

"Ugh." But Bella couldn't believe Rafe thought of her as a sister anymore. "I wish it were that simple."

Amy's concerned expression warned Bella she wouldn't like what was coming next.

"As long as I've known you, you've had a dream," Amy said. "A little thatched cottage in the country with a big garden and a husband and a whole load of babies."

"I know. That's not changed. I'm just going to manage it without the husband. I can do this on my own."

"Not entirely on your own. Why couldn't you have picked someone a little…easier?"

"Maybe because I couldn't see myself doing it with anyone else. Actually, I couldn't see myself doing it with Rafe. Not until the kiss."

"Hmm, well, at least his reputation is good. Despite the fact that he appears to change his women more often than I change my hair color, there's no scandal I've ever heard."

"How do you know all this?" Bella asked.

"The paper has a file on him."

"Really? Why?"

Amy shook her head in exasperation. "Do you know nothing? He's one of the richest men in the country. He had family money, but he's made billions since he took over Santini's."

"I've never really thought about his money before." Bella tugged on the end of her plait. All that money made her uncomfortable, but at least she understood his lawyer's reaction a little better now. Why couldn't Rafe be more… ordinary?

Amy patted her knee again. "Strange child. Anyway, in business he has a reputation as being totally ruthless."

"He told me that when he took over, he had to prove

himself."

"And boy, did he do that." She took a sip of wine. "So you want to go ahead with this?"

Bella nodded.

"And you don't want to go down the artificial insemination route? You know, it could save you a whole lot of heartache."

"Rafe won't break my heart. He's my friend."

Amy had a doubtful frown, but then she clapped her hands. "Okay, so…seduction. The first thing you've got to realize is that men think with their dicks."

"Then why won't he touch me?"

"Well, probably because he's trying very hard not to."

"He won't even see me alone. He gets this slightly panicked look on his face when I suggest he come up to my room."

"Poor Rafe. I could almost feel sorry for him. Almost, but not quite. So as I said, his natural tendency is to think with his dick. You've got to use that."

"How?"

"You have to make him aware of you as a woman all the time. But be subtle. You're beautiful—"

"I am? I—"

Bella was interrupted by her cell. She nearly ignored it. It could only be Rafe, and she'd told him last night that she was spending the evening with Amy.

It rang again. She couldn't resist hearing his voice.

"Bella."

"That's me."

"I have to leave."

"Oh." She couldn't believe the disappointment that washed through her. She crushed the phone to her ear waiting for him to continue.

"There's a problem with the Hong Kong deal."

"And only you can sort it out?"

He was silent for a second. "It's the way I live."

She gnawed on her lower lip. "Thanks for letting me know. When do you have to go?"

"Now. I thought you might come to the airport with me. My driver can bring you back."

She glanced across at Amy. "I'm with Amy, I…" Amy was making frantic hand signals in her direction.

Go, she mouthed.

Bella frowned but nodded. "Can you pick me up here?"

"I'll be there in fifteen minutes."

"Now's your chance," Amy said when she ended the call. "He'll be alone with you in the car. Not that much can happen while he's driving."

"He's not. He has a driver."

"Even better." She rubbed her hands together. "He'll never expect it. Not in the back of the car."

"He'll never expect it, because it's never going to happen."

"Come on, I'm not suggesting you go all the way or anything. Just a little bit of foreplay. You've got a chance. Then all the time he's away, he'll be thinking of you. Now, how long have we got?"

"Fifteen minutes."

"Well, let's get going. We have a lot to do…"

"Makeover?"

"The fastest one ever. So strip," she said, her words muffled as she rummaged in the wardrobe.

After that, things moved too fast for Bella to have much say in the transformation taking place. She viewed herself in the mirror as her friend set up her equipment and tried to absorb the constant stream of Amy's seduction tips.

"Is this what he wants?" Bella asked ten minutes later.

"I'm just bringing out your best qualities."

"These are my best qualities?" She glanced down at her breasts, prominently displayed in a black lace half-cup bra.

She'd never considered herself well-endowed before, but pushed up and sticking out like this, they were impossible to ignore. "You don't think I'm being too obvious?"

A look of mock alarm crossed Amy's face. "There's no such thing—believe me, men like obvious."

Bella shut up after that and just did what she was told.

• • •

Why was he here? The thought crossed Rafe's mind as he stood on the doorstep and waited for someone to answer. Why wasn't he on his way to the airport instead of interrupting her evening?

But he didn't know how long he would be away. And he wanted to see her. That bothered him.

But it was too late now. Footsteps approached down the hall inside, followed by a feminine giggle. But no one was laughing when the door opened. He recognized Amy, though they'd only met once at Bella and Gary's wedding, and that day he hadn't taken notice of much. Too busy fighting his private demons.

"Hi, Rafe."

"Hi." But he was looking beyond her for Bella.

Bella came to stand beside her friend and his eyes narrowed. Something about her looked different, but he couldn't pinpoint what. For once, her hair was loose, tousled, framing her face, but it was more than that. The night was warm, but she had some sort of shawl wrapped around her. What was she hiding?

He'd miss his plane if they didn't get a move on, so he didn't take time to wonder. After saying his good-byes to Amy, he ushered Bella to the car and into the back.

"So, you're off to Hong Kong?" she said as she settled into the leather seat.

He nodded.

"Don't you hate that?"

"Hate what?"

"Just getting up and going halfway around the world."

"I love it."

In the dim light, he could see her brows draw together as though she didn't understand. But the truth was he did love the traveling, loved waking up in the morning in a new country, on a new continent.

At the same time, he realized that this once, he didn't want to go. He wanted to stay and spend more time with Bella. Keep an eye on her. He supposed there was an alternative.

"You should come with me sometime," he said.

"What, to Hong Kong?" She sounded surprised.

"Or New York. Or Sydney...wherever."

"I don't know. I'm a stay-at-home kind of girl." As she spoke, she ran a hand through her hair, tousling it even more.

"You might enjoy it."

"Maybe. But I doubt I'll be able to soon." Her hand moved from her hair to rub her lower lip.

Rafe tried not to stare. "Why?"

"I'm starting job interviews tomorrow." One finger stroked down her throat, and he had to force himself to concentrate.

"I can give you a job."

She shook her head. "I don't want you to give me a job. I want to get one on my own."

"You won't be able to work if you have a baby."

"I'll worry about that if it happens."

"What sort of job?" He wasn't happy about this job thing but didn't understand why. It was what he wanted—some sign that she was taking control and moving on with her life.

"You know I've been working at an online degree in modern languages since we moved to Spain. Well, I finished earlier this year and want something where I can use that. I'm seeing a career adviser, but I'm also signing on with a couple of temping agencies, so I should get something quite soon. That will keep me going while I look for something long term."

It made sense, but he still didn't like it. Why not work for him? He'd think about it when he was alone. Come up with some options.

He relaxed and studied her. Since she'd answered the door, he'd been trying to figure out what was different about her. Makeup. She was wearing makeup. Not a lot, and the effect was subtle, but even so, quite devastating. The black smudged under her eyes made them look huge and almost silver in the muted light. And lipstick. She nibbled her lips and then licked the lower one with the tip of her tongue. Heat shot through him, settling in his groin. He had a sudden mental image of that lush red mouth around his dick, and he shifted uncomfortably on the seat. He had to stop thinking like this.

Bella waved a hand toward the tinted glass partition separating them from the driver. "Can he hear us?" she asked.

"Not unless I press the intercom."

"Oh."

She was up to something, but what?

Sitting in the corner, half facing him, she crossed and uncrossed her legs. She wore heels, black strappy sandals. And her legs were bare, and there was a lot of them. She crossed them again.

Beneath that shawl thing, she wore a skirt or a dress, he couldn't tell which. Whatever it was, it was short. He hadn't seen her in a skirt since she'd arrived in London. She always wore jeans for him.

He shifted again on the seat and decided he needed to get his mind off the skirt. One more thing to add to his list of things he shouldn't think about. "So how was your friend?"

"Amy? She's good."

They lapsed into silence again.

"It's warm, isn't it?" she said.

Was it? Hot, more like it.

She let out an exaggerated sigh and started to unwind the black shawl.

Fuck.

At least he hadn't said the word out loud. She was wearing a dress. Almost wearing a dress. It covered just about nothing. She inched a little closer to him and he fought the urge to back away. There was nowhere to go.

"Actually," she murmured, "I thought while we were together like this, we could discuss this artificial insemination idea of yours."

Not likely. Thinking of insemination at this point, artificial or otherwise, was not a good move.

The dress was low cut, and her breasts were pushed up and out from the top in a way that was almost indecent. How come she dressed like that to visit a girlfriend? She'd never dressed like that for him. But then why should she? He was the man who'd suggested they never ever have sex.

Had she said something else? "Sorry?"

"Artificial insemination. You remember?"

"What about it?"

"Well, obviously there are some advantages, but—"

"But?" He realized he was talking to her cleavage and dragged his eyes up to her face.

"The thing is, I'm an old-fashioned girl. And I wanted this to be a fair exchange. You said you wanted me and..." She twisted further in her seat and leaned toward him, raised her hand, and rested it on his chest beneath his jacket. He could feel the warmth of her skin through the thin cotton of his shirt.

"I totally get it if you've changed your mind and don't want me like that. I'm not gorgeous and sophisticated like your normal women."

What the hell was she talking about?

"Rafe, couldn't you just..." She gave a helpless look. "Close your eyes and pretend I'm beautiful?"

He didn't know what to say. So he kept quiet.

"Am I really so repugnant?" She blinked. Were her eyes glistening? Had he done this to her? Made her cry?

"That's not why... I thought you wouldn't want... Shit, Bella."

He dragged her into his arms and onto his lap. He meant only to comfort her. But the feel of her, the sweet scent of warm woman so close, was too much. His hands slid beneath her hair, and his mouth slanted over hers.

For a second, her lips remained clamped. His tongue slid along the line separating them, and she gave a soft sigh and parted for him.

She twisted on his lap and just like that was straddling his hips with their mouths still fused. His dick was rock hard, and he couldn't help himself. He pushed the straps down over her slender shoulders, then tugged the dress so it pooled around her waist. And sat back.

Black lace.

Half cup.

Her breasts spilled over, her nipples peeking from behind the lace. For a moment, his eyes feasted on her. Then he lowered his head and kissed the smooth golden skin.

• • •

The touch of his lips sent darts of pleasure racing through her as he scattered kisses across her breasts. Bella glanced at the panel that separated them from the driver. The glass was tinted, she could only see him as a shadow, and she pushed him from her mind.

She closed her eyes and gave herself up to the wonderful sensations coursing through her body. She'd never experienced anything like this, the cool whisper of his breath against her skin, the warmth of his mouth melting her insides.

Rafe was hard beneath her, and she lowered herself to press his erection to her core. Pleasure coiled inside her, starting a deep ache low down in her belly. With his hands splayed across her back, he urged her forward. Then he bit down on her nipple through the lace of her bra, and her back arched, her sex flooding with heat. He bit down again and her lids flew open.

Bright lights.

Streetlights lined the road as they passed under a huge sign. Crap, they were almost there, and the car was slowing as they drove into the airport.

She dug her fingers into Rafe's silky hair and tugged.

"Rafe!"

Finally he got the message and raised his head. His eyes were heavy-lidded and sleepy, filled with the desire she'd wanted from him.

"Bella…" His hands tightened on her waist and she tried to push them away.

"We're there, Rafe." She recognized the moment he came back to himself. Groaning, he ran a hand through his hair. At least he looked mussed now.

They pulled up in front of the departures building, and he gave her breasts one last look before dragging the straps of her dress up over her arms. He slid his hands back to her waist, picked her up, and placed her beside him. Then he rested his head back against the seat.

Chewing on her lower lip, she waited for him to say something. She couldn't resist a quick glance down; the evidence of his arousal was still clear to see.

"I'm sorry. That shouldn't have happened." He took a deep breath. "And I'm fed up with saying that."

"Maybe you're wrong. Maybe it's supposed to happen."

The driver was out and had stepped around the back. She followed his movements as he pulled Rafe's bag from the trunk and then opened the car door. Rafe would be leaving any moment, and she wanted to say something, anything. She just didn't know what.

He climbed out, then leaned down toward her. "We'll talk when I get back."

She stared after him until his tall figure disappeared into the airport.

In the rear of the car, returning to the city, Bella tried to analyze their encounter.

It had actually gone exactly to plan.

So why didn't she feel like celebrating instead of like a manipulative little bitch?

Her body still tingled from his touch, and she was damp and hot. She'd never expected to feel this way. Oh, she'd presumed he would be a competent lover; after all, he'd had mega-loads of practice. But this ability to make her lose herself in sensation was scary, and unanticipated, and she didn't know how to deal with it.

And right now, she couldn't shake the nagging sense of guilt, the uncomfortable sensation that she was way in the wrong.

They'd been friends, but on a superficial level, because she'd never tried to see the real Rafe beneath the glamour.

Now she saw him clearly. And the truth was, she liked him. Rafe wanted her. She could see that, but for whatever reasons, he'd decided he couldn't have her. However, those reasons would have her best interests at heart, because Rafe was an honorable man. She could only presume he'd told her the truth—that he didn't believe she was ready for a relationship with him. Or for a baby.

He was wrong about the baby. She deserved that baby, and she would be a good mother. The best. Her child would never want for love.

But maybe he was right about the relationship—Rafe had the potential to overwhelm her. How would she feel when they parted, as he'd warned her they inevitably would? The problem was, she didn't see how spending more time with him would help. In fact, it was clouding the issue. The more time she spent with him, the more she wanted him. Maybe it was because it was all so new. Until Rafe, she'd never even kissed a man other than Gary.

She groaned. It was official—she was a sex-crazed widow. But she wouldn't try to seduce him again. It wasn't fair. Instead, she would tell him how she felt. Maybe he'd give her a pity fuck and her hormones would settle down and she'd stop thinking about sex.

She buried her head in her hands.

She so wasn't looking forward to that conversation.

Chapter Nine

Looking lean and handsome in his uniform, Colonel Sinclair was seated at the hotel bar when Bella entered. The last time she'd seen him had been at Gary's funeral, though he'd written to her many times since. In the past, she'd never felt entirely comfortable with him. He'd been against their marriage, and she'd presumed he thought she wasn't good enough for his son—her father was a lowly sergeant, while Gary was an officer's kid.

She'd just finished her shift at her temp job showing foreign tourists around the sights of London. Her feet hurt, and she was desperate for a drink. Rafe had been gone four days, and she missed him. He'd finished in Hong Kong but had slotted in a trip to Singapore afterward. That's where he was now, or at least where he'd been when he called last night.

He called her every evening. They kept the conversations light and impersonal. So far, they'd avoided mentioning the trip to the airport.

In the meantime, she had a long to-do list to keep her busy, and seeing Gary's father was close to the top.

He was nursing a drink, his large hand clasped around the glass. When he saw her, a smile flashed across his face. He appeared genuinely pleased to see her. Her steps faltered. He had the same blond hair and gray eyes as his son, and a shaft of pain shot through her.

As she approached, he rose to his feet and held out his arms. She was surprised, but stepped forward and returned his hug.

After a moment, he drew away. "Can I get you something?"

"A glass of red wine, please."

He ordered the drink and then turned back to study her. "You look more beautiful than ever. Gary was a lucky man."

Again he surprised her, and she answered without thinking. "I believed you never thought I was good enough for him."

He shook his head. "Honey, I knew you were too good for him. I loved Gary, but you were more woman than Gary could handle by the time you were fourteen."

Bella sank onto the barstool beside him. This wasn't how she remembered things. The bartender placed a glass of wine in front of her, and she sipped it to give herself time to think.

"I was a skinny tomboy. I was surrounded by men, and not one of them ever looked my way."

He laughed. "Poor Sam."

Sam was her father, Sergeant Samuel Deacon. "What do you mean?"

"Do you know what he threatened to do to any man who looked your way? What he threatened to do to every new guy on the base?" He chuckled. "I don't think he slept a single night after you turned fourteen. You didn't help. You were a wild child."

"Not that wild," she muttered.

"We used to laugh about it. Sam could control a whole

barrack full of squaddies, but one little girl had him running in circles."

Bella's mind reeled.

"So yeah, I was a little concerned about you marrying Gary. I didn't think it would last." He shrugged. "I wasn't sure he could make you happy."

"He did."

He patted her knee. "I know. And you made him happy. I spoke to him a few days before the accident. He was so proud about the baby. I just wish that baby had happened."

She glanced away and bit her lip as tears stung her eyes. "So do I."

"A piece of Gary. Still, it wasn't to be." He sat on the stool beside her and picked up his drink. He was giving her time to pull herself together, and she appreciated his concern. She hadn't realized how much seeing him would hurt. Or maybe she had, and that's why she'd avoided even thinking about him.

This man brought back the past so vividly, and remembering those times left her feeling lost and inadequate, and she hated that.

Her dad had been a member of the elite Special Air Services—her mother had said she left because she couldn't live with the constant fear. But that wasn't the case. Her mother had been so beautiful. She'd wanted parties and excitement, to be admired, none of which she'd gotten from Bella's dad, who was posted overseas for long stretches of time. So she'd left, reluctantly taking Bella with her—a four-year-old wasn't the sort of accessory her mother desired.

She'd died five years later, driving back from a party, three times over the legal alcohol limit. Bella's dad had taken her after that, and from the start, she'd been a pain.

"So what are you doing in London?" Colonel Sinclair pulled her from her thoughts.

She bit her lip. "I'm with someone."

"A man?"

She nodded.

"I'm glad," he said. "I worried about you alone at the farm. It's no place for a young woman."

"I wasn't ready to leave."

"And are you now? You know, Gary wouldn't have wanted you to live your life alone."

Maybe her determination to stay on the farm had been some sort of penance. Perhaps she felt guilty that she hadn't loved Gary more, or loved him better. Rafe had made her realize the one thing missing from her marriage—passion.

Being with Rafe had changed everything, including how she viewed her marriage. She hadn't known she could feel desire like that. Rafe only needed to look her way to set the fires inside her alight.

For the first time, she wondered whether she'd have been content with Gary forever. She'd married him because he was the best person she'd ever met and they both wanted the same things from life. She'd known he'd never let her down, never leave her.

Except he had.

Maybe if they'd stayed on the farm, away from temptation, the feelings of restlessness, the idea that life was passing her by, would have faded to nothing once she'd had the baby and a real family around her.

She just didn't know anymore. Didn't know who she was.

"So this man—is it serious?" the colonel asked, and she thought about her answer for a moment.

"Not really. We're more friends than anything else." She shook her head. "Rafe doesn't do serious."

His eyes widened. "You're with Rafael Sanchez?"

She nodded. "Are you shocked?"

"No, not shocked. Gary once said the only way you

would ever leave him was if Rafe decided to have you. And he reckoned Rafe would never do that."

Her mouth fell open. She placed her glass slowly on the bar. "Gary said that?"

"Hmm. After I'd told him you were too young, that you couldn't know your own mind. He told me I was wrong. So, are you happy with Rafe?"

"Well, I'm not sad. That's something. But it's not like… that. Not yet, anyway."

"You're a sensible woman. You'll sort it out. Now, how about we finish our drinks, then go get something to eat and you can talk to me about Gary."

"I'd love that."

• • •

Where the hell was she?

Rafe had called from the airport, but there was no answer from the hotel room, and her cell phone was obviously switched off. He'd even tried the damned PA, and the stupid woman hadn't a clue where Bella was. What did he pay her for?

He needed a drink.

But when he entered the hotel bar, he saw her straightaway. She sat on one of the tall stools at the bar, her long jeans-clad legs crossed, a glass of red wine in her hand. Her hair was loose, a cascade of dark fire down her back, and his lips curved up in a smile as he stepped toward her.

His smile froze. He came to a halt just inside the door, his eyes narrowing at the sight of Bella placing her hand on another man's arm. She turned so she sat in profile and smiled at him.

Rafe forced his gaze from Bella to the man at her side. He had his back to Rafe so he couldn't see his face, but he was tall and wore some sort of army uniform. From the silver in his hair, he was also considerably older than Bella, but that didn't seem to prevent her from pawing him. What was she doing picking up soldiers in bars?

She reached up and kissed the man on the cheek, and Rafe felt a growl building up inside him.

Mine.

He was about to storm up to the couple, punch the man, toss Bella over his shoulder, and carry her off, no doubt beating his chest in a Neanderthal-like manner, when the officer turned his head. Rafe recognized him immediately. Gary's father. He stopped his forward momentum in midstride.

Rafe couldn't believe the strength of his over-the-top reaction. He was in trouble, and it was time to put a stop to this. During his time away, he'd come to the conclusion that he needed to tell Bella the truth.

That he could never give her a baby.

He didn't want to lie to her any longer. He fingered the box of condoms in his pocket. He'd fought a losing battle, and it was time to give in. He'd offer her a no-strings affair and see where they went.

Bella wanted him—maybe not as much as he wanted her, but she couldn't fake her reaction to him.

So maybe it was time they gave in, had an affair, and got the inconvenient attraction out in the open and out of their systems.

His affairs never lasted. While not breeding contempt, familiarity tended to lead to disinterest. Part of him knew that would be for the best, and they could part amicably and Bella could move on. The rest of him hated the idea.

Of course, there was always the risk that once they'd made love, he'd never want to let her go. He'd worry about that when and if...

Breathing out, he relaxed his facial muscles, formed them into a smile, and stepped forward.

Bella must have sensed his approach and turned slightly, her eyes widening as he approached. "Rafe." She sounded breathless. She removed her hand from the other man's arm, slid off the stool, and came toward him. "I wasn't—"

He leaned down and kissed her, cutting off the words. It was a kiss of pure possession. *Mine.* The word whispered through his mind as she melted against him, her fingers clenching his shirt, her mouth opening beneath his as their surroundings faded from his consciousness.

Someone coughed, and Rafe pulled away reluctantly. He looked past Bella, and his eyes caught the older man's. A flicker of amusement flashed across the colonel's face.

"Not serious, huh? Looks pretty serious to me," he said to Bella, and then turned to Rafe. "Hello, Rafe."

Rafe frowned at the "serious" comment. He raised one eyebrow at Bella, but she just shrugged. "Sir." He held out his hand and the colonel shook it, his grip firm, his gaze searching Rafe's face.

"It's good to see you," he said.

"You too, sir."

"Now, I'm sort of standing in as Bella's father, and I suppose I should be asking what your intentions are," the colonel said, then he smiled. "But maybe I'll wait until you've worked that out for yourselves. It's time I left." He turned to Bella and kissed her forehead. "I think maybe we'll take a rain check on that meal." He glanced at Rafe as he spoke, a challenge in his eyes.

Some small part of his brain urged him to tell Bella to go ahead with her plans and have a meal with her father-in-law. No doubt they had things to talk about. But he couldn't get the words out. Instead he stood, silently willing the other man to leave.

A look of wry amusement entered the colonel's eyes. "Don't be a stranger," he said to Bella.

"I won't."

"Good. I'll see you again before you leave? There's something I need to talk to you about."

"Of course."

Why the hell couldn't the man just go? Finally, he nodded at Rafe, and then strode out of the room.

Rafe watched until he disappeared before turning back to Bella.

She glared at him. "You weren't very friendly."

"I don't feel *friendly.*"

Her eyes widened. "You don't?"

"No."

"What do you feel?"

Rafe allowed some of his hunger to show as he studied her out of half-closed eyes. She shifted under his attention. *Good.* "Why don't we go up to your room?" he asked. "And I'll tell you. Maybe even show you."

For a moment, she appeared to sway toward him, and then she frowned and stood up straighter. "Actually, I'm hungry. Could we stay down here and get some food?"

"We can order room service." Lobster and champagne. He'd feed her. Afterward.

Her frown deepened. "I need to talk to you about something."

Her words brought him out of his nice little fantasy. And reminded him. He also had things he needed to talk about. She looked serious, and panic flared inside him. Had she decided to leave?

Well, if that was the case, what he had to say would hardly persuade her to stay. "I have something to say as well."

Five minutes later, they sat across from each other in the hotel restaurant. The waiter approached.

"Are you ready to order?" Rafe asked.

She shook her head. "Later. After we've talked."

Rafe waved the man away, then called him back and ordered a scotch for himself and another red wine for Bella. He sat back in his seat, tried to relax, and waited for her to speak. She was nervous. Her eyes were darting around the restaurant, and she was drinking way too fast.

"Tell me," he said when he could bear the suspense no longer.

She bit her lip. "I wanted to apologize."

Relief filled him at her words. At least she hadn't said she was leaving. Followed by confusion and a hint of panic. What did she need to apologize for? What the hell had she done? Had she found some other man to give her a baby? He took a sip of scotch and waited for her to continue. When she remained silent, he decided it was up to him. "What for?"

She chewed on her lower lip, positively gnawing on it. At another time, the sight might have distracted him, but right now he needed to hear what she had to say. She took a deep breath and then spoke very quickly. "I set out to seduce you in the car that night."

He blinked a couple of times while he processed that information. "You wanted to seduce me?" he asked slowly. That wasn't so bad.

"It was premeditated—I asked Amy how to make you want me, because I believed now that you'd actually spent some time with me, you couldn't face the idea of making love. But afterward I felt so bad and horrid. You're doing what you think is right, making me take my time, and I'm trying to push you."

"Let me get one thing straight. You tried to seduce me to get pregnant?"

She glanced away. Then back. Raised her glass to her lips, then realized it was empty and put it down. "Yes...no.

God, this is so hard. I do want a baby, desperately, but I also want you. I hadn't realized I would, but I can't stop thinking about sex. With you. Is that normal?"

He shook his head, pressed his fingertips to his forehead. She wanted him. But she also still wanted the baby. The baby he could never give her.

"You can't stop thinking about sex? With me?" He asked because he really needed her to say it again.

"Yes. But it was your fault. You kissed me."

"All this because of one little kiss."

For the first time, anger flashed in her eyes. "It wasn't a little kiss. And before you kissed me, I'd never thought of you like that. It had never occurred to me that there could ever be anything between us. I—"

"Did you want something between us?"

She rolled her eyes. "No. Not then. But I wanted a baby, and then you kissed me, and I thought you wanted me, and I thought why not? And then in the hotel you kissed me again and touched me and ever since..." She scowled. "Well, since then, I think I've made my feelings *embarrassingly* plain on that subject."

"In retrospect, the whole back-of-the-car thing was a little obvious, but I wasn't thinking clearly at the time. Not with my head, at least."

"I noticed." She fiddled with the stem of her wineglass, and then looked him directly in the face. "So anyway. I needed to say sorry. And I won't try to seduce you again."

He really wished she hadn't said that. "Pity."

Her eyes widened. She opened her mouth, but at that moment the waiter approached and refilled her glass. She took a sip. "What did *you* want to talk to *me* about?"

God, could he put this off? She wanted him. Would it be so wrong to give her what she desired? Tell her later. Much later. But he knew he couldn't go forward without being honest. "I lied to you."

"You did?"

"I never intended to go through with the baby deal. I just wanted to stop you from rushing into something with someone else. I'll never have children."

"Why?"

For a second, he seriously considered telling her the truth, but in the end, he couldn't make himself. The need for silence had been instilled in him at too young an age. One day, he might. But it wouldn't be tonight.

"It's not relevant. But believe me. I will never have children."

She searched his face. "So where do we go from here?"

"Where do you want to go?" He knew where he wanted to go. Straight to bed. But he could see the confusion in her eyes. "I do want you, Bella. More than I've ever wanted anyone."

"And if we have an affair, how long will it last?"

"I don't know. As long as we want it to." He reached across and took her hand, glanced at it and back to her face. "You've taken off your wedding ring."

"It was time."

He didn't know how that made him feel. Sad in a way, but happy she was finally moving on. "You know, Gary used to talk about you long before you married—he said all you ever wanted was a husband, a home, a family."

"That makes me sound very boring."

"Never. But I believe one day you'll want that again. And maybe some time with me will help you heal. Help us both heal from Gary's death." He pushed back his chair. "But I don't want this to be about Gary. I want it to be about you and me. Right now I'd love to take you to bed and lose myself in you. Show you how good it can be between us. But I'm going to leave you to think about things. Call me when you know what you want."

He rose to his feet and was about to turn away when she spoke.

"Tell me one thing. You want me, really want me?"

He nodded.

"Since when? When did you first know?"

"From the moment I met you."

Chapter Ten

From the moment I met you.

Bella hugged the pillow to her. Even hours later, the warm, fuzzy feeling was still there. It seemed Rafe had been suffering a case of unrequited…lust all these years. Evidently, he was an extremely good actor.

Then the warmth faded as she remembered what else he'd told her. He'd lied. He'd never had any intention of letting her have his baby. All the same, he'd gone to an enormous amount of trouble for that lie. Bringing her over here, keeping her company, that whole contract thing. Obviously he'd been trying to protect her in his alpha-man crazy way. And she'd pushed him into it by flirting on the farm when he'd been there. He was trying to save her from herself.

He wants me.

And there was that heat again, spreading through her body until she positively glowed.

Damn, she wanted him, too. So much it scared her.

During the long, sleepless night, she had reached a decision.

He claimed he would never have children. Part of her didn't want to believe him, but mostly she sensed his conviction. But why was he so sure? And could she convince him to change his mind? Because somewhere along the way, she'd gone from wanting a baby to wanting Rafe's baby.

She'd tried to convince herself that it was because he was the closest thing to Gary, but she knew that was no longer the case. And Rafe was right. She hadn't really gotten over Gary's death.

Living at the farm, with so many memories and so few distractions, it was unsurprising. Only by putting some distance between her and the place had she really begun the healing process.

Rafe claimed his relationships lasted three months. Would that be enough? It had to be. She was going to make a leap of faith and just hope it would all work out.

She finally fell asleep somewhere before dawn and woke not many hours later to a delicious feeling of contentment.

Rafe wanted her. He'd been fighting it, but now he'd given in. And if she had her way, today he was going to get her.

First, she had things to do.

A knock sounded at the door, and she glanced at the clock. Too early for Sally. It was probably one of the hotel staff. Hotel living was not for her. The sooner she got out of this place, the better.

She dragged herself out of bed, pulled on the robe, and went through into the living area. She opened the door to Rafe.

"I wanted to check that you were okay."

She glanced down at herself. She was a mess. Not okay at all. It was her day off, and she'd planned to spend the afternoon making herself gorgeous and sexy and alluring and then call him. Instead, she was in her pajamas, with bed hair and sleep in her eyes.

"I thought you were Sally," she mumbled.

"Sally?"

"My PA, remember? Actually your PA, really." She stepped aside and gestured for him to enter. Then took her first good look at him and realized he didn't appear much better. Mr. Perfect was rumpled, and she bit back a smile. He wore the suit he'd had on last night. His tie was gone, the shirt open at the neck; his hair was mussed, his eyes slightly bloodshot, and stubble shadowed the hollows of his cheeks.

"Wow," she said. "You look a little..."

He ran a hand over his chin. "Rough?"

"Just a little."

"I called John—lawyer John—last night after I left here. We went for a drink, actually a few drinks, and I ended up sleeping on his couch." He glanced around. "I don't suppose there's coffee?"

"I'll order some." She studied him as she called up room service. She liked him like this. He looked incredibly sexy and bad-boy with the dark shadow and heavy-lidded eyes.

"Why's your PA coming here on a Saturday?" Rafe sat on the arm of the sofa.

"So far I've been a huge disappointment for her, poor thing, but yesterday, I actually came up with something for her to do."

"And that was?"

"She's been apartment hunting for me. She's come up with a whole list—she's frighteningly efficient—and we're going to go through them this morning and maybe visit some possibilities this afternoon. Though she wasn't very hopeful— apparently I can expect something the size of a small garage for what I'm willing to pay, and I'll probably have to share that."

She'd considered looking for a place outside the city, because London was exorbitantly expensive, but she didn't want to move too far away from Rafe. The apartment was likely only short-term anyway. She'd been for a first interview and had the possibility of a really good job. But the company was international, and if she was accepted, she had no clue where she'd be based. She couldn't turn the job down if she was offered the position, but she was trying not to think about what that would mean.

"Why do you need an apartment? Aren't you happy here?"

She rolled her eyes. "It's a hotel room. Granted a very nice hotel room, but it's hardly a home."

He still looked confused.

"Okay. The truth—the place is driving me nuts. It was great for a novelty for a few days, but now I feel like I'm in a goldfish bowl. And I want to make a mess."

"And you can't here?"

"No, it all gets picked up before I even get started. And if I want a coffee, I have to call down. And…" She plucked at her pajama top, unsure how to explain it to man who hardly stayed in one place long enough to unpack. "I just want some space of my own."

He jumped to his feet. For a moment, she thought he was leaving, and she took a step forward, her hand reaching out as though she could stop him.

"Come on, get dressed," he said. "Well?" he asked when she didn't move.

She frowned. "Well, what?"

"You don't like the hotel, and I'm not happy about you getting some dingy apartment in the wrong part of town. So the solution is—you'd better come home with me."

Had she heard that right? "Home? With you?"

"Don't worry—it's a big house. You can have your own room, make as much mess as you like."

"I can?"

She realized she was doing her parrot imitation and clamped her lips together as she tried to get her head around his offer. Did she want to go home with him? She wanted to get out of the hotel. But to live with Rafe? She wasn't the easiest person to live with—chances were it would cut her three months down dramatically.

"I thought you never lived with anyone?" she asked.

"Doesn't mean I can't. I should have offered earlier, but I thought you liked it here."

"I'm quite messy, and I'm betting your house is as perfect as you are."

"Not a problem, I have a"—he hesitated for a moment—"a housekeeper. He can look after you when I'm not there."

"I'm not totally useless, Rafe."

"He can still look after you—make him feel useful. And he cooks, though you're quite welcome to cook if you want to."

Her insides were tingling, and not just with the idea of getting out of the hotel. To catch a glimpse of the real Rafe, see how he lived. She might discover some interesting insights into what made him tick. See him in his natural environment. Get him into bed. Sounded like a plan. She nodded once, then disappeared into the bedroom.

• • •

Rafe stared at the closed door. What had gotten into him? He'd never taken a woman to his home, let alone invited one to stay. But it seemed like the right thing to do. Before he could change his mind, he picked up the phone and called his driver.

At least this way he could keep an eye on Bella. Hopefully, more than an eye.

Telling her the truth had lifted a weight from him. He

couldn't have made love to her with the lies lingering between them. Though he was concerned that she still believed there was a chance he might agree to father her baby, but that could never happen. He'd accepted that fact long ago, but maybe he'd accepted too easily, given up too soon.

He still held his phone in his hand; now he flicked through the numbers for one he'd never called before. He stared at the name for a minute, then took a deep breath and pressed the call button.

"Professor Erskine?"

"Yes?"

"I'm sorry to bother you during the weekend. We've never spoken, but my name is Rafael Sanchez, I'm—"

"The man who funds my research," the professor finished for him. "It's no bother. Just don't tell me you're pulling funds."

"Not at all. In fact, I'd like to meet with you and discuss increasing your funding. And a more...personal matter. Perhaps you could come to my office on Monday."

"Of course."

"I'll see you at ten, then."

He ended the call and shoved the phone in his pocket. His heart was beating fast, which was stupid. The meeting would probably come to nothing, anyway. But at least he was covering all bases. At least he was trying to give Bella what she needed.

And if he failed, then maybe he could show her there were better ways to live than in the confines of marriage. He could show her his world, what life could be like unfettered by the chains that tied other people. She could travel with him. And they'd split the rest of the time between London and New York. Visit his grandfather, too. He could stand the place with Bella at his side.

The water ran in the bathroom while she showered,

and he thought about joining her. But she'd said her PA was expected soon, and when he got Bella naked this time, he didn't want any interruptions.

The coffee arrived, and he was on his second cup by the time she came out. She'd dressed in her usual jeans, but with a pretty camisole top that showed off her bare shoulders and offered flashes of her flat, tanned stomach. Her hands were shoved in her pockets.

"So where is this house? Is it far?"

"Not far. It's in Belgravia. I've called for the car—it will be here in five minutes."

"But I have to pack."

"No need. You can phone your PA from the car and she can do it and bring your things over." Suddenly it was important to get her out of there before she decided she preferred a dingy apartment to a room in his house.

• • •

The car pulled up into a large underground parking area, empty but for some sort of low-slung black sports car.

The driver got out and opened her door. Bella tried to shrug off the feelings of intimidation she always experienced when faced with overt demonstrations of Rafe's wealth. He lived right in the center of London. This place had to be worth millions. Perhaps she didn't want to stay here, after all. It was becoming clearer why Rafe's lawyer friend had worried about her getting her claws into him.

"What's the matter?" Rafe asked from beside her.

What was she supposed to say—that he was too rich? They came from such different worlds. She was way out of her depth, and the thought sent a shiver of unease through her. So she shrugged off his question and scrambled out of the car.

Rafe led her across the garage to an elevator that took them up a single floor. The doors opened into a large reception area, and a man stood in the center of the huge room as though waiting for them. He appeared to be somewhere in his late fifties, his dark hair turning gray, and he wore a black suit and stood ramrod straight.

Rafe tilted his head toward him. "This is Charles. He runs the house. If you need anything, just let him know."

The man nodded. "Mrs. Sinclair. I've prepared the blue room for you as instructed."

"You have?" So she wasn't going to be sharing with Rafe. Which was good. She'd have her own space.

"I'll show her around, Charles."

Bella glanced back over her shoulder as Rafe ushered her away. "He's not a housekeeper," she whispered. "He's a butler. You have a *butler*?"

Rafe winced at the question. "I inherited this place from my grandfather—my maternal grandfather. Charles came with the house. What was I supposed to do—throw him out?"

She grinned. "You're embarrassed. Admit it. That's why you called him a housekeeper. Should I tell him?"

"God, no. Actually, he's brilliant and cooks like a dream."

The place was all marble floors and antique furniture—it looked more like a show house than a home. Or a show mansion. A number of double doors led off the hallway, but Rafe ignored these and led her instead up a wide stairway. He came to a halt outside a door.

"This is your room."

He pushed open the door for her and stood to the side while she passed him. The room was perfect, beautiful, decorated in creams and blues, a large vase of irises on a small table by the door. Charles had been busy. And it was large—even larger than the hotel room.

"You can make as much mess as you like," Rafe said.

"I'm not sure I'd dare."

He ignored her muttered comment. "You have your own bathroom, through there—" Rafe nodded toward a single door in the far wall. "And I'm close by."

"You are?"

"Yes." He strolled toward a set of doors in the far wall. "This house was built in the days when husbands and wives had separate bedrooms, but in this case they're connected. Mine is through here." He threw open the doors to reveal an even bigger room beyond. Unlike the rest of the house, this room screamed modern, which she guessed was more Rafe's tastes. Decorated in black and white, it was the ultimate in sophistication. An enormous bed stood on a platform in the center. An image flashed in her mind of Rafe sprawled there golden and naked, and her heart rate picked up.

"It suits you," she said.

He closed the door, and Bella gazed around her at what she presumed was to be her home for the foreseeable future. "It's beautiful."

He turned to look at her, a small frown on his face. "You don't sound impressed."

"I am. Very. It's just not very…homey."

She kicked off her sandals and dug her bare toes into the soft carpet, then crossed the floor to stare out the window. They were at the front of the crescent-shaped row of houses. A green area of park directly in front of them, and beyond that the city. Miles and miles of buildings, and she had a sudden longing for the wide-open mountains of Spain.

"Are you all right?"

Rafe's softly spoken words interrupted her thoughts. He leaned against the wall, his eyes narrowed, arms folded across his chest.

"I'm fine. I just…" She gestured to the room around her. "It's different than I'm used to. I guess I'm feeling a little homesick. I don't fit in here." She would never fit in his world. It was like a shower of cold water on her heart.

"You can fit in anywhere."

"You're sweet." She lifted one shoulder, trying for a nonchalance she didn't feel. "Anyway, it doesn't matter. I'll just enjoy the luxury while it lasts."

She realized that neither of them had brought up their conversation of last night. Then again, just by bringing her here, he demonstrated that he still wanted her.

Rafe watched her, a slightly wary expression on his face. She had the urge to smooth the lines between his eyes. She took the few steps to close the distance between them.

"Thank you for offering to share your home with me."

"My pleasure."

"I hope it will be."

She needed the reassurance of his arms around her. She could do this. Rising on tiptoes, she burrowed her head into the curve of his neck, breathing in the sharp, clean blend of warm man and expensive cologne. Her body recognized the scent of him and reacted to the memory of other times they had been close, growing hot and heavy. Her breasts ached, and a slow pulse started between her thighs.

She lifted her head and rubbed her lips against the roughness of his cheeks. "Hmm, prickly."

"I need to shave and shower. Come with me?"

He threaded his fingers with hers and led her into his bedroom. Once inside, she tugged at his hand and turned to face him. She didn't want to wait. Her body craved his touch, hungered to be filled. The feelings were so new, and she felt lost, off-balance, needing his touch to ground her in this new world. "Kiss me, Rafe."

Sliding his hands under her hair, he tilted her head and lowered his mouth to hers. The kiss was everything she remembered, hot and hungry. Her whole body tightened as his tongue pushed into her mouth, sliding against her tongue, and she melted from the inside.

He raised his head. Desire burned in his eyes as he plucked open the buttons down the front of her camisole, parting the material and slipping it from her shoulders. Bella lost the ability to think as his hands slid across her skin, up over her rib cage, to cup her breasts. Her skin flushed, sensitive; her nipples hardened to tight little points. His long, tanned fingers framed her curves, and Bella had never seen anything so sinfully erotic. Then he trailed a finger over one swollen pink nipple, and her body clenched with desire, a pulse starting between her thighs. Reaching up, she clutched his shoulders for support as her legs went weak and a wave of heat engulfed her. He kissed her slowly, his tongue thrusting leisurely into her, while his clever hands played with her breasts until she was a mindless mass of quivering need.

She hardly noticed as his hands went to her waist, opening the buttons of her jeans. He pushed them down over her hips without ever breaking the kiss.

• • •

The blood thundered in his veins, and he ached viciously to be inside her.

But he was sure there had been no one since Gary; he needed to take things slow though every cell in his body screamed to take her fast, make her his, show her how it could be between them.

Without releasing her mouth, he stroked his palm over the flat plane of her stomach and flirted with the curls at the juncture of her thighs. Her jeans were in the way, and he pushed them lower. She wriggled and kicked free of them to stand before him naked. For a second he stared, unable to take his eyes from her—he'd wanted this for so long. Then he cupped her in his palm, pressing upward, and she stilled in his arms. He rotated his hand against her softness and felt her melt.

"Oh." She whispered the word against his lips.

Rafe raised his head and stared down into her wide-open eyes as he slowly slid one finger between the folds of her sex. Something relaxed inside him as he encountered the evidence of her arousal. Hot and slippery with desire, and his fingers glided over her with ease. He found the opening to her body and dipped one finger inside. She was so tight, her muscles clenching around him, and he had to fight for control as a wave of raging lust washed over him.

Sliding his moistened finger up to find the small bundle of nerves, he teased her lightly, taking note of her reaction. Her lashes fluttered, and a slightly panicked look entered her eyes. "I don't...I can't..."

But despite the protestations, her hips pushed toward him. He shifted her so one arm supported her around the waist. Pushing his middle finger inside her, he stroked the swollen nub with the pad of his thumb, and she fell apart in his arms.

He held her close as she jerked against him. As the tremors subsided, he touched her lightly, and she came again so sweetly.

He fumbled between their bodies and freed himself. Then he reached into his back pocket, pulled out the foil packet, tore it open, then quickly rolled the condom over his erection.

Glancing up, he found her gaze fixed on him, eyes wide. "I've been like this for the entire past week," he said. "And if I don't get inside you soon, I'll likely go insane." Unable to wait any longer, he backed her against the wall, grasped her hips, and lifted her. "Wrap your legs around me."

Her long legs clasped him around his waist, and her

scorching heat pressed against him.

He slowly pushed himself inside her, and the feeling was so fucking good. He paused when he was in as far as he could go, sighed against her skin. "You okay?" he murmured.

Her face was flushed, her eyes half closed, dazed, but she gave a small nod. He started moving inside her, shoving in and out of her slick heat, his hands holding her firmly in place, his eyes, then his lips, playing over her naked breasts, her face.

Her lips were slightly parted, her breaths short and fast. Part of him said to go gentle, but her hips bucked against him, urging for more. His speed increased until it was wild, the pressure building at the base of his spine, spiraling out of control, and he knew he was close. Moving one hand between their bodies, he stroked the most sensitive part of her until she exploded around him, her muscles tightening on his cock sending him tumbling headlong over the edge. Her lips parted in a scream, and his mouth came down on hers, silencing her, as raw pleasure flooded his system.

Afterward he slumped, head in the curve of her neck, her legs still around him, as his heart slowed to normal. He didn't want to move, it felt so right, but the position couldn't be comfortable for her.

Slowly he pulled away, lowering her to the ground and grabbing hold of her arms as her knees gave way. He picked her up and carried her to the bed.

"So much for taking things slowly," he murmured as he sank down to the mattress with her still in his arms.

• • •

The frantic beating of her heart steadied. Slowly, Bella became aware of her surroundings.

She licked her lower lip—it was tender from his kisses.

Little tremors of pleasure still rippled through her body, and she clamped her thighs together. She'd never known it could feel like this. Already she longed for more.

She was naked, cuddled on his lap as he sat on the bed leaning against the headboard, long legs stretched out. "You didn't even take your clothes off."

"I got carried away." He stroked the hair back from her face. "Are you okay?"

She gave a weak laugh. "I'm not sure 'okay' covers it."

"I know it's been a while for you. I should have been gentler. But, *querida*, you don't make me feel gentle."

When he said *querida* in that husky voice, little shivers ran through her.

Would she ever get enough of this?

Chapter Eleven

Rafe worked long days, disappearing from their bed in the early hours. But he spent the evenings with her, and they ate dinner together in the small informal dining room, as opposed to the huge formal one that looked like it seated at least fifty. Mostly, Rafe would talk and Bella would listen. She loved listening to his voice. The topics were varied and impersonal, on purpose she presumed, but made her realize how cut off from the real world she'd been in Spain.

And he touched her all the time, little gestures he didn't seem aware he made. A hand at her waist. A finger stroking her cheek. She warned herself they meant nothing, but she found herself waiting for them.

And afterward, they'd go to his huge bed and make love.

She never thought she'd get enough of him.

In bed or out.

She spent her days showing Spanish and French tourists around London and making friends with Charles. She'd also been to a doctor and sorted out contraception—whether they had a baby or not, it wouldn't be yet. On the fifth day, Rafe arrived home early.

"I've brought you a present," he said as he came through the door into the sitting room where she was curled up on the huge sofa reading. Bella sat up and waited for him to produce a jewelry box, or something similar, the refusal already hovering on her lips.

"It's in the kitchen with Charles," he continued.

In the kitchen? A coffeemaker perhaps? Her own personal freezer? Everything she came up with seemed highly unlikely. Curious, Bella followed him out and down the hallway.

In fact, the kitchen appeared empty, Charles nowhere in sight. She paused just inside the door and looked around. Then down, and found her present.

"He's called Toby," Rafe said. "I know you like dogs. I thought he could keep you company."

A dog. Rafe had bought her a dog. Toby was small, with black wiry fur and beady brown eyes that regarded her anxiously. He was actually quite ugly.

"He's not a puppy, but I thought you'd prefer an animal from the rescue center instead."

Her gaze shot to his face. "You went to a rescue center to get me a dog."

"Yes, and for a while there, I thought they weren't going to hand him over. Apparently, they do house checks, and I wasn't a good bet as I'm out all day. I told them the dog wasn't for me, but they said if he was living in my house… In the end, I explained about Charles."

"And that worked?"

"Well, that and the donation."

Bella stared at the little dog as he sat between them on the flagged kitchen floor, gazing up at her. She couldn't believe he'd bought her a dog.

Crouching down, she reached out a hand, and Toby

licked her fingers.

"I know he's not the most attractive dog ever, but apparently he'd been there a while and…"

"You felt sorry for him."

Rafe ran a hand around the back of his neck and looked vaguely uncomfortable. "Something like that. But we could take him back and get you a pedigree puppy if you'd prefer."

Bella picked him up and cuddled him close to her chest. "Don't you dare."

She'd had a dog in Spain. A stray who'd adopted them as soon as they moved in, but he died last year, and she'd missed him terribly. She'd been waiting for another to turn up as they always did where she lived.

Toby would have loved Spain. As long as he didn't get too used to living in luxury in Belgravia, he'd be okay. She had a momentary worry about what she'd do if her job came through. But she pushed it aside. Time to worry about that after the interview. Amazingly, the company had called her back for a second meeting in a few days' time. She hadn't yet mentioned it to Rafe.

"Thank you."

She stepped close to Rafe, leaned up, and kissed him on the cheek, with the little dog between them. "It's the nicest present anyone has ever bought me."

Rafe shook his head. "Well, I did consider a diamond necklace, but I thought you might throw it in my face, and I wanted to give you something you could love."

Charles appeared at that moment carrying a huge pile of doggy equipment, a bed, leads, blankets, bowls. He placed it all on the table and turned to face her. As usual, she had no clue what he was thinking.

"Where would you like them?"

"In my room, please."

"Wouldn't the kitchen be more suitable? Or the garage

perhaps?"

She grinned. "Probably, but I'd still like him in my room."

"I thought he'd keep you company," Rafe said.

She glanced up from cuddling Toby. "You're going away again." It wasn't a question. He'd warned her, but still she couldn't believe her disappointment.

"I have to go to Rome tomorrow."

"How long?"

"I'm not sure. You could come with me. Do some sightseeing. Visit the Colosseum. We could go together."

For a moment, she seriously considered it. But she had work tomorrow, and the second interview coming up. She couldn't take off. She needed to get her life in order—this was very likely a time-out, and she shouldn't forget that. "I have to work. Besides, I can't leave Toby alone so soon."

He shrugged, seemingly unconcerned. "Okay."

• • •

Four days later, and Rafe still wasn't back. After Rome, he'd headed for Madrid. She missed him desperately, even though he called her each day. And that scared her. Maybe she wasn't the sort of person who could sleep with someone and not feel emotion. She remembered Rafe's warning that this would change their relationship. And he'd been right. She doubted she could ever go back to thinking of him as just a friend. So where did that leave her? Would she have to cut him out of her life when their affair was over? Just the thought made her queasy.

She passed the time, though. Amy had come for dinner one night, and Charles had served them in the huge formal dining room where they'd giggled uncontrollably through the whole meal. But he had refused to let Toby sit at the table.

Afterward, Bella had taken Amy on a tour of the place,

including the swimming pool and gym in the basement. Amy had been very impressed. They'd ended up in Bella's favorite room—the wine cellar—drinking a bottle of red Charles assured them wouldn't be missed.

"So how's it going?" Amy had asked.

"I don't know," she replied. Though truthfully, it was more that she was trying not to think about the future. Just living in the moment. Which was new for her and left her feeling as though she balanced on the edge of a precipice.

On the morning of the fifth day, Rafe phoned to say he'd be back that evening. It was also the day of her second interview. If she was successful, she'd have to talk to him about her new job and the fact that she'd very likely be leaving.

• • •

"Mrs. Sinclair, could you come in please?"

Bella stood, smoothed the skirt of Amy's little black suit, and went back into the office.

"We'd like to offer you the position. Starting next month."

Bella waited for some sort of emotion. But she felt numb.

"This is a management training program and as discussed, you will be expected to spend time in our other offices. You'll have a month of orientation in London first, and then you'll move to our head office in San Sebastian for a year. I take it that's still not a problem."

Was it?

With the starting date they'd mentioned, the end of that first month in London would just about coincide with Rafe's three-month time limit for a relationship. Would he even want to see her after that? Maybe this was for the best. A good clean break. She tried to ignore the stab of pain to her heart. She had to be strong.

"Of course," she murmured.

The job was perfect for her. She could use her languages, and it was an excellent opportunity for someone with no experience. She should be really happy.

And she would be. One day. Soon. Maybe.

They spent half an hour going through details. Bella tried to take it all in and not to think what having this job might mean.

She switched her phone on as she stepped outside. There was a message from Gary's father asking if they could meet, and she punched in his number.

"I have to go away for a while," he said. "I wondered if you had time to meet for a drink. There's something I want to talk to you about."

She planned to meet Rafe in a bar close to his office. But she had an hour before he'd arrive, so she arranged to meet the colonel there.

"Call me Mark," the colonel said as he led her to the table.

She glanced at his face. "I'm not sure I can."

"Well, try. You can't keep calling me colonel." He grinned. "You could always call me dad."

The idea boggled her mind. "I don't think so, *Mark*."

The table was situated in a small window alcove, and Bella sat and stared out onto the street, watching the people walk past. It felt weird sitting here with Gary's father. He'd been such an authority figure when she was younger, which had always increased her underlying need to behave badly.

"You look fabulous," he said. "Positively glowing. So how are things going with Rafe?"

Bella wasn't quite sure how to answer. What was she supposed to say? *The sex is out of this world, but it's only temporary.* It hardly seemed an appropriate comment to make to one's father-in-law. She broke off a piece of breadstick and nibbled it while she attempted to come up with a more politic answer.

"Okay. But his life is just so different."

"He's rich. Very rich."

"I know."

"You don't sound happy about it."

"It doesn't really affect me so I try to ignore it. But…" She shrugged. "That sort of wealth is unreal—I can't even begin to comprehend it, so I don't try."

"Yeah, you can buy anything with that sort of money."

She glanced at him sharply. Was he going to accuse her of going after Rafe's money as well? "He hasn't bought me."

"I never said he had," Mark replied. "But you're not his usual type."

Bella snorted but decided not to comment.

"What?" he asked.

"Well, you're not the first person to mention that." She studied him for a moment. "Did you think I married Gary for his money?"

Shock flared on his face. "Never."

"So it really was just that you thought we were too young?"

"That, and you were a little wild."

It was true. Though maybe "little" was being kind. Now she could see she'd been hurting. "My dad didn't want me," she said. "I guess I was making him pay."

The colonel regarded her, one eyebrow raised. "Why would you think that?"

"My mother told me…" She trailed off. "My father refused to take me, even for holidays." She could still remember the pain those words had caused, spurring her to make her father pay.

"If she told you Sam didn't want you, then she lied. God, that woman was a bitch. It's good you take after Sam and not your mother."

"I do?"

"Yeah. Did you know your dad tried to get custody of you when your mother left him?"

"No." This meeting was rewriting history. Why had she never questioned what her mother had said after the divorce? She shook her head. "Oh God, and I was so horrible to him."

"I think he enjoyed it. Used to call you a chip off the old block, said you would have made a great soldier—apart from the fact that you were crap at taking orders."

"I never did what he told me on principle—I was a brat."

"Well, Sam was the same—he was busted down to private more times than anyone I know. He could never do what he was told—but all the same he was a great soldier; his men loved him."

She'd known that, and underneath she'd loved him as well; she'd just never been able to forgive him for not wanting her. And all the time she'd been wrong.

"Holy crap. I was so bad. And I led Gary astray. I made him get a tattoo and—"

He laughed. "Maybe you'd better not tell me any more. I don't want to lose my rosy image of my son."

"You wouldn't. Gary was one of the good guys."

"I know." He was silent for a moment and then released his breath on a sigh.

Bella sipped her wine and thought about what he'd told her. Her childhood had shaped who she was and what she wanted out of life—a home and a family. Now she realized those needs were based on an interpretation of facts that weren't true.

Had she been wrong about everything?

Rafe's way of life was different from anything she had ever known, but that didn't mean she couldn't adapt. But then there was still the fact that he didn't want a long-term relationship—he'd been brutally honest about that. They never spoke of the future, but she presumed that hadn't changed.

"What are you thinking about so seriously?" Mark interrupted her thoughts.

"Do you think I made a mistake mixing myself up with Rafe?"

"Well, I'm certainly not going to tell you not to continue seeing him."

"You're not?"

"If I remember rightly, telling you not to do something was a guaranteed way of getting you to do it." He grinned. "Sam used to say it was the only way to get you to do anything he wanted. He just had to be careful not to use it too much."

Bella's eyes narrowed.

"With regards to Rafe—to be honest, I don't know. But Rafe is an honorable man." He patted her hand. "I guess just try not to get your heart broken."

"I won't," she said. Though she wasn't sure that was the truth. She suspected her heart was already in dire danger. She went still. That was the first time she'd admitted to herself that her heart was involved. Rafe had been right— underneath, she still wanted the same things—a home and a family—and he wouldn't give her that.

"There was another matter I wanted to talk to you about," Mark said.

"There was?"

"It was something I was discussing with Gary at that last meeting we had."

Bella frowned. "He never mentioned anything."

"I'd told him I was releasing his trust fund. He was planning on buying half the farm from you. He always felt bad that you'd put up all the money."

"He shouldn't have."

"Maybe not, but he did, and I was happy to help him. I

worried when you married, but you'd been together for four years, you had a baby on the way, and I realized I'd been stupid to think you wouldn't stick it out. You might have been flighty, but once you set your mind to something you were committed the whole way. Then he died before the paperwork went through, and for a while I just couldn't think about it."

"Gary asked you for this?"

He shook his head. "No. I offered. It was Gary's money, though—left to him by his mother. He just couldn't get to it without my releasing the trust fund. I'm going to do this, Bella. It's what Gary would have wanted. I should have done it before now, but as I said—I wasn't thinking straight after Gary died, and then I just let it slide."

"So why now?" she asked. "What's changed?"

"Nothing. That's the point. Gary was your husband. He should have put as much into the marriage as you did, and you'd have been left with a nice little nest egg to help you survive when he was gone."

"I've survived all right. And I've actually just been offered a job. A good one. Well, it won't pay much for the first few years, but it has prospects."

"This will give you something to tide you over for those first few years."

She bit her lip. The money would help.

Sitting back in her chair, she thought about Mark's offer and her future. Deep down, she suspected no one else would ever rouse the passion she experienced with Rafe. She had a hunch that what they had together was unique. But even if he didn't tire of her, if he never offered her anything more, would it be enough?

Somehow, she'd find the strength to move on, get a life, and for now, a career. Mark's offer would help her do that, and he was right—Gary would have wanted her to have the money. It would also mean she could keep the farm. She'd been ignoring how much the thought of selling it, losing all those happy memories, hurt because she had no choice. This gave her one, and it would also pay for a better place to live, with a garden for Toby, and a dog walker when she was out all day.

She'd allow herself the weeks until she had to move to San Sebastian, and for that time she'd work to find a way they could be happy together. But while there were things she'd compromise on, there were other dreams that she wouldn't surrender. An image of that beautiful blue-eyed baby flashed through her mind.

"I can almost see your brain working." Mark's words interrupted her thoughts, and she glanced up. "So, have you come to any conclusions?"

Lines of tension settled around his eyes as though he'd geared himself up for a fight. She smiled and reached across the table for his hand. "I'm thinking…thank you."

Some of the tension left him, but he frowned. "That was too easy."

"Maybe I'm mellowing in my old age."

"That must be it. I'll finalize the paperwork tomorrow and probably drop round with some things for you to sign." His head cocked to one side as though debating something in his mind. "You know, I always thought you might join the army—like your dad."

"What?" She hadn't expected that suggestion. Not from this man. "You know how crappy I am at taking orders."

He grinned. "You were always pretty good at giving them, though. You could consider officer training. I'd put in a good word for you."

"You would?" She still reeled from the notion of her being in the army. It was a stupid idea.

"The army is a home of sorts—it gives you a place to

belong, and I know you've always needed that. Anyway—think about it."

"I will."

"Are you aware your boyfriend has arrived?" Mark asked.

"He has?" She stiffened as a tingling ran between her shoulder blades. She turned slowly.

• • •

Rafe sat on a stool at the bar nursing his drink and trying not to make it too obvious that he was staring at Bella across the busy bar like some lovesick idiot.

But idiot just about described him. He hadn't been entirely sane since he'd kissed Bella all those months ago.

God, he'd missed her. He'd almost cut his travel short and come home.

Now she turned to look at him, and a smile of welcome curved her lips.

Without hesitating, he rose to his feet and strolled over. He placed his glass on the table and sank into the seat next to Bella. Leaning over, he kissed her lightly on the mouth. "Hi," he murmured and searched her face. Had she missed him?

She wore a black suit and black high heels. He'd never seen her looking so smart. Was this for her father-in-law?

"Mark was just suggesting I join the army," she said.

Mark? Since when had Gary's father become "Mark"? And join the army? Over his dead body!

"It was just an idea," the colonel said. "But think about it if you decide against that job. Now I'll leave you alone, but I'll drop those papers at the hotel tomorrow morning."

"She's not at the hotel," Rafe said. "She's living with me."

The colonel raised an eyebrow. "In Belgravia?"

Rafe nodded.

"Okay, I'll drop them off there." He rose to his feet. "Have a pleasant evening." He turned to go, then paused. "Look after her," he said to Rafe.

"I will."

"Why does everyone think I need looking after?" Bella asked as he disappeared. "I have actually managed quite well on my own, you know."

"He feels responsible for you."

"Well, he shouldn't."

No, he shouldn't, Rafe silently agreed. Bella was his responsibility now. But he wisely kept the words to himself. "So what is this job?"

"I've been offered a management training position with an international company where I can use my languages."

"Which company?"

"SA International. You know it?"

He nodded. The company was solid. So why didn't he like the idea of Bella working for them?

"I'll be based in Spain for a year."

She said the words so nonchalantly that at first they didn't sink in. "What?"

"In San Sebastian."

"When?"

"I start at the beginning of September. I have a month's orientation in London, then I move."

Never going to happen. The words hovered on the tip of his tongue, but he bit them back. Being with Bella was giving him a crash course in thinking before he spoke.

"And what's this paperwork?"

"Mark is releasing Gary's trust fund to me."

"He is? About time." But he felt a niggle of unease at that bit of news as well. It was as though she were distancing herself from him. He should have felt happier about that; instead he felt disconcerted, off-balance.

"It means I won't have to sell the farm."

"I'm glad." But was he? Maybe she needed the break from the past in order to make a new start.

"Toby missed you," she said.

He didn't want the goddamn dog to miss him. He wanted that from Bella.

Suddenly he needed her alone. In his bed. The one place he knew he could reach her. He raised his gaze to her face and found her watching him. Her cheeks flushed as she held his stare, and he knew she wanted the same.

It was enough. For now, it had to be.

She rose to her feet and held out her hand. "Let's go home."

Chapter Twelve

Rafe rolled onto his side and glanced sleepily at his watch. It was ten o'clock in the morning, and he was still in bed. His body felt heavy and sated with too much sex. Though he doubted there was such a thing as "too much" where Bella was concerned.

Out of bed, she was guarded, edgy, often sharp-tongued with quick comebacks. But once in bed, the sharp edges smoothed away and she was all soft, sensual woman. He'd never met a woman who gave in to sensuality with such abandon.

She was out of bed now, though. Wrapped in a fluffy white robe and sitting cross-legged in a chair, she studied him out of half-closed eyes.

He came up on one elbow. "What are you doing over there?"

"I was watching you sleep."

He shifted, uncomfortable with the idea. "You were?"

"Hmm. Shouldn't you be at work? Aren't you a 'busy' man?"

"Work can wait."

She raised a brow. "I was going to paint my toenails. But I can't decide on the color." She picked up two bottles, one a lurid neon orange, the other bright banana yellow. "What do you think?"

"Nice colors." *Not.*

"I think so. I went shopping with Sally yesterday at lunchtime. She wanted me to get this scarlet stuff. She tried to tell me it was sophisticated, but really, it was just tarty. She said it would go with the stilettos you bought me." She studied the bottles. "I think I'll go with both, but should it be one foot each or alternate nails?"

He didn't have a logical answer to that one. Instead, he watched as she rested one bare foot on the edge of her seat and applied the polish, the tip of her tongue poking out between her lips as she concentrated.

"Bugger. You know, there's more on my toe than there is on my nail. Who would have thought the whole nail polish thing could be such hard work?"

"Come here, *querida*." He patted the bed next to him. "I'll do it."

"You will?" She tilted her head to one side. "Okay."

Bringing her bottles, she came and sat on the bed facing him. Rafe lifted her foot to his mouth and kissed the inside of her ankle, his hands stroking the silky skin of her calf, the sensitive spot behind her knee. For a second she lay back, her lashes drifting closed, then she came up on her elbows and eyed him.

"Hey, you're supposed to be working." She pushed the bottle into his hand, and he took it from her and rested the foot on his thigh. Her feet were beautiful, with high arches and slender toes. He painted each nail carefully.

"You're good," she said. "Do you do this often?"

He grinned. "No, it's a first."

When he'd finished, she changed feet and handed him the second bottle, the yellow. For a moment, he thought about arguing, then shrugged. As he unscrewed the top, his cell phone rang from the bedside table. His heart tripped a beat as he recognized the number. He glanced warily at Bella, then put down the bottle and picked up the phone. "Professor Erskine?"

"I have the information you asked for."

Rafe's mouth went dry, and he swallowed. "And…?"

"Would you like me to come in tomorrow and talk you through it?"

"No. Tell me."

The professor was silent for a moment. "It's not good news, I'm afraid. There are no options right now, not if you want absolute certainty."

His chest tightened, and he realized how much he'd been holding on to hope. "Thank you for letting me know."

"Don't give up—we're making huge progress in this field."

"I won't. Send me a full report."

He ended the call and placed the phone back on the table.

"Is something wrong?" Bella asked.

He shook his head and forced a smile. "No. Just work."

After all, the news was nothing he hadn't expected. He wouldn't give up, but he would put it from his mind and concentrate on the present.

He picked up the yellow polish and carried on. After the last toe was painted, he put the bottle on the table and sat back. "It's my mother's birthday next week," he said. "She's having a party." His words surprised him; he hadn't intended to mention his mother's annual, totally over-the-top party. "Will you come?"

A frown flickered across her face. "I don't have anything to wear."

"Well, you'll have time to get something." As he spoke, he realized how much he wanted her to accompany him.

"I'm not sure. I was sort of thinking that if I stay under the radar, then your sister might forget all about me and, you know, the whole…'I'm having your baby' thing."

He'd avoided thinking about the encounter with his sister. He'd also avoided his mother's calls and his stepfather's, and anyone else from the family who'd phoned. Gina would have told everyone, and he didn't want to answer the questions bound to follow. "I doubt that very much."

"Well, I don't want to cause you any more trouble with your family."

"You won't. And my mother was fond of Gary. She'd like to meet you."

"Hmm. So why do *you* want me at this party?" she asked.

"Because I enjoy your company?"

"Won't your family think it odd?"

A small frown flickered across his face. "Why?"

"Well, it must be a close family affair."

"A close family affair for five hundred."

"Five hundred people! Your mother invites *five hundred people* to her birthday party?"

"Give or take a few."

"Wow. There I was thinking we'd be sitting around a table stuffing ourselves with birthday cake."

His lips quirked. "Not quite."

He wished they could hide away from the world for the foreseeable future, but he couldn't avoid his mother's birthday celebrations, and he wanted Bella with him. He had a strange feeling time was running out, and the call from Professor Erskine had only intensified that feeling. In the week since he'd been back, Bella hadn't mentioned the job again, and he didn't know whether she'd accepted the position. He didn't want to ask. Didn't want to find out she was leaving him.

But how could he ask her to stay? He had no claim on her. He'd told her that was how things had to be. Nothing had changed, but maybe it was time to rethink his position, to confess his motives for avoiding marriage and children and see where they went from there. His guts clenched at the thought. No doubt once she found out, she would leave him, but the uncertainty was driving him crazy.

After the party. He'd give himself another week.

Bella sat deep in thought, her lips pursed. "I'll think about it."

He decided not to mention that the party was in New York. He'd tell her later. After she'd said yes. "Are they dry?" he asked nodding toward her toenails.

"I guess."

"Good." Clasping a hand around her ankle, he tugged her up the bed toward him.

• • •

As the frantic pace of her heart slowed, Bella rolled onto her side so she could study the man at beside her. Rafe sprawled on his back. One arm was flung over his face, hiding his eyes, and his olive skin gleamed with a fine sheen of sweat. His lovemaking had been fierce, wild, exhilarating, and with just a hint of desperation.

Her body was sated, boneless, but a niggle of worry prodded at her mind. He'd changed after that phone call, though he'd tried to pretend it wasn't important. She hated that he felt he couldn't share. That he kept huge parts of his life from her.

She'd made an effort not to think about the future. But she only had two weeks until her job was due to start. Then another month until she'd have to leave for San Sebastian.

So many times she'd considered talking to him about what

would happen when she left. Every time, she had backed off, scared of where it might lead. And each night he made her forget her concerns. He could make her forget everything. It was only when they ventured outside that life intruded, so she tried to keep those times to a minimum, content to spend their evenings at home. But she was quite aware she was hiding from real life, and that couldn't last forever.

His desire for her had shown no sign of waning. If anything, he seemed to want her more, and the feeling was mutual. He intoxicated her. He had only to walk into the room and her every cell was instantly aware of his presence. As though her body recognized him, knew him, grew languorous and heavy when he was near. But it was more than that. She liked just being with him. She missed him when he was at work. Listened for him returning in the evening.

The intensity of her emotions terrified her. And she'd avoided putting a name to those feelings.

By now, she knew he cared. While he never spoke of his feelings, they were clear in his actions. She just wasn't sure how *much* he cared. And if it was enough to break through whatever barriers he had put up between them. Barriers she was pretty sure he believed insurmountable.

Were they?

How the hell was she supposed to know if he wouldn't talk to her?

At the start, Rafe had told her categorically that he would never marry, never give her the family she wanted, and he'd said nothing since to suggest he'd changed his mind.

She didn't think he would want them to part after three months. But what did that mean? Did she just stick around indefinitely, hoping that one day he would want more from her? What if that never happened? She would have the choice of saying good-bye to her dreams or walking away. The former made her heart ache, but the latter caused actual physical pain. She had lost one man she loved. Did she want to live through that again with Rafe?

Man she loved?

The world stopped. She sat bolt upright in the bed.

Oh dear God. I love him.

Beside her, Rafe lowered his arm and pushed himself upright. "Are you okay?" Her gaze darted around the room to avoid looking at him.

She freaking loved him. What the hell was she going to do?

"Bella?"

She cleared her throat. "I'm fine." She searched her mind for a distraction. "So tell me about your family. Who'll be at this party? You know it's weird, I've known you all these years but you never talked about them."

He raised an eyebrow, but sat back. Obviously, it wasn't a simple request. "Gary was more my family than anyone."

"Why?"

He shrugged. "There was a ten-year age gap between the rest of the children and me. They were close, but I never really fit in with them."

"Aw, that's sad."

"Not really." He was silent for a few minutes. "What do you want to know?"

"Anything. Everything."

"If I tell you will you come to the party?"

"Maybe." She wasn't agreeing to anything. Meeting Rafe's mother would traumatize her no matter the situation. In the normal course of things, she'd likely never meet the woman, but if she went to this party, she couldn't be avoided. And Bella's comment to Gina would only make the occasion a thousand times worse. "If I go to this party, is your mother going to be weird about the baby thing?"

"Yes. But don't worry, she's not about to whip out a

pregnancy test and demand you take it."

Her eyes widened. "Oh my God, I hadn't even thought of that option. Maybe Gina won't have told her."

"She'll have told her, and yes, probably she's going to be…surprised."

"Surprised? Why? Doesn't she expect you to have children one day?"

"No. She knows I won't ever marry. She probably believes she set such a bad example that I would be put off forever."

Was that a warning? She ignored it, because he was actually opening up, and there was so much she wanted to know. "Oh. And did she? Tell me about how your mother and father met. I've heard all the gossip from the villagers in Spain, but you must know what really happened."

"My mother was on holiday in Spain when she met my father. She was eighteen. He was nineteen. As far as I understand it, they had a wild holiday affair, and my mother ended up pregnant. With me."

"And they married?"

"Yes. According to my mother, they were in love. But my grandfather was against the wedding—he said they were too young. There were other reasons, but he didn't tell us those until after my father was dead."

What other reasons? She wanted to ask, but he was already speaking again.

"Apparently he nearly convinced my father not to go ahead with the wedding—I don't think my mother has ever forgiven him."

"But they did marry?"

"Oh yes, and it turned out my grandfather was right. One of my earliest memories is of them arguing."

"They didn't get on?"

"In some ways, but they wanted different things. My mother wanted more children. My father didn't." He stared straight ahead, deep in thought. "They argued about that all the time. But maybe it was just an excuse. I've no doubt they were in love, but they were too different. They came from different worlds, and in the end I wasn't enough to hold them together."

His words sent a shiver of unease through her. "What happened?"

"He left when I was eight. Went back to Spain, but he died of pneumonia a year later. My mother never forgave him for leaving or for dying. But she married my stepfather a year after that, and I think she's been happy."

"That's good." It was a sad story and maybe one that went a long way toward explaining Rafe's views on marriage and commitment. But that only increased her fears for the future. "Your grandfather must have been devastated by your father's death."

"I was too young to remember, really. But I'd guess so. He was his only son and only twenty-eight when he died." He shook his head as if to dispel the memories. "Enough talking about my family. If you come to the party you can meet them for yourself." He cast her one of his sexy smiles, and her insides melted. "How do you fancy lunch in Paris, and this afternoon I have a hankering to kiss you on top of the Eiffel Tower."

She frowned. "How do we get to Paris?"

"I can have the helicopter ready in an hour."

Her mind was still churning from her realization of just how far her feelings for Rafe had gone. She'd think about the love thing later when she was alone, and soon she must make a decision about the future. But she'd never been in a helicopter. Or to Paris. As a distraction it sounded perfect.

"I'll go get dressed."

• • •

It was five long days since her momentous realization that her life had derailed. Contrary to everything she had promised herself after Gary's death, she was head over heels in love. With a man who would never marry and with zero chance of a happy ever after. She was twitchy, on edge, and every time she thought about the future, her stomach roiled. She couldn't live like that. Not long term without some sort of commitment. She'd be a basket case.

Rafe had noticed. She occasionally caught a concerned look in his eye, but he was ignoring it. He was so good at ignoring things he didn't want to talk about.

She hadn't meant to do this now, had wanted to put off the moment as long as possible in the hope she might get some sign from Rafe that her feelings might one day be reciprocated.

So far a big fat nothing.

And he'd been pushing her for an answer about the party. He'd asked her again at breakfast. She'd replied she hadn't decided.

But for the first time, and quite irrationally, her anger had risen. She was a woman in love. With a man she was sure didn't believe in the emotion. She was allowed to be irrational. She'd silently fumed as he kissed her on the top of her head and said good-bye.

She didn't want to go to a goddamned party. Didn't want to meet his family. And why did he even want her to, anyway? She was nothing to him. Well, maybe that wasn't true. But he didn't want her to be any more than she was now. Certainly didn't want her love.

After he'd left, she'd smashed a cup, and then bawled her eyes out, shocking the hell out of both Charles and Toby.

"Hormones," she'd muttered, which had only increased the fear in Charles's eyes. In that moment she'd come to a decision. She was going to give Rafe a way out. This had to end. She'd confront him. Tell him she was leaving. It would be the hardest thing she had ever done, but she couldn't do this any longer.

So here she was.

The elevator opened to reveal Peter North, working at his desk in front of the double doors leading to Rafe's office. Bella hesitated, her finger twitching with the need to press the down button, get the hell out of there.

Don't be a wimp.

She took a step forward as Pete glanced up from his desk and grinned. "Hey."

She blew out a breath. She could do this. "Hi, Pete. Any chance I can I see Rafe?"

"He's in a meeting right now, but I'll let him know you're here."

She paced the room as he picked up the phone, spoke quietly. Maybe he'd be too busy and she could go away and rethink this whole thing. But less than a minute later, the double doors opened and there he stood in all his corporate billionaire perfection. She glanced down at her faded jeans and T-shirt. How had they even gotten this far? They were too different. But why did he have to be so goddamn gorgeous?

He smiled. Then his smile faded as he studied her face as he came forward. "Bella, are you all right?"

She gave a jerky nod. "I just needed to talk to you."

"Come in here." He led the way through a door to the left of his office and into a small meeting room with an oval table and eight chairs. She crossed to the window and stood staring out over the city. Rafe came up behind her and rested his hands on her shoulders, pulling her back against him.

No way could she do this while he was holding her, and she turned around and pulled free, took a step away.

His brows drew together. "What do you need?"

"I don't *need* anything." She shuffled from foot to foot

not knowing how to start. First things first. Then work her way up to the harder stuff. "I'm not going to the party."

"You're not? Why?"

"I can't go."

"You mean you don't want to go."

"Maybe. I'll be leaving soon and..." She shrugged. "I don't see the point."

His eyes narrowed. "You're leaving? I thought you had weeks before you move to Spain."

"I do. But the job starts next week, and they've offered me corporate accommodations for the month I'm in London."

His eyes narrowed. "You don't need accommodations in London. You have accommodations."

She forced herself to continue. "It was good of you to put me up. Get me out of that hotel, but I know you like your own space."

"I don't want you to go," he ground out.

"We'll still be friends."

"Goddamn it, I don't want to be your fucking friend."

She took a step back from the ferocity in his voice. "Then what *do* you want, Rafe?"

He stared at her for long seconds, then turned away, one hand raking through his hair, tension radiating from his body. Finally he came back to her. "Just tell me why."

"You said right at the beginning, we want different things. My time with you has been fabulous, wonderful, beyond anything—"

"Then why go?" He rubbed at the spot between his brows. "Why not stay?"

"Because it's not enough."

Pain flashed across his face. "You still want the home and family?"

"I can wait, but yes, one day I want a baby." God, she wished she could tell him she loved him, but it felt too much like emotional blackmail. He'd never asked for her love. She hardened herself to what she had to say. "But you don't. And you've made it clear you're not going to change your mind. I have to think about the future. I need to move on and we're"—she gave a helpless shrug—"we're not going anywhere."

She'd been looking somewhere over his left shoulder; now she forced herself to focus on his face. It was wiped clean of expression, giving no clue what he was thinking. Her eyes felt hot and scratchy, her mouth dry while she waited for him to say something. Anything.

Not a word.

"Oh God, I can't do this anymore." She whirled around and headed for the door, blinking back the tears. She so did not want to break down until she was away from here and on her own.

"Don't move out," he said as her hand reached for the door. "Not yet."

She turned slowly.

"Just give me a little more time. Stay at the house until I get back from New York."

"You're going to New York?" she asked.

"For the party."

She shook her head. "Your mother's party is in *New York*?"

"I was going to tell you as soon as you said yes."

She sighed, the strength oozing out of her. "I won't leave until you get back." Though she was pretty sure there was nothing to wait around for. Rafe would never change.

• • •

Rafe winced as the door clicked shut behind her, tightness wrapping around his chest like barbed wire.

Sinking into the chair behind him, he stared at the spot

where she'd disappeared. He rubbed at the back of his neck, trying to ease the tension.

He'd failed, lost her.

And it had been nobody's fault but his own.

Now all he could hope for was the chance to explain. Maybe that way, at least she wouldn't hate him.

Chapter Thirteen

"He's gone, Toby."

The little dog peered back at her with his beady brown eyes.

Bella sniffed, took another gulp of red wine, before resting the nearly empty bottle carefully on the stone floor beside her. "You can stop wagging your tail. It's nothing to be happy about."

In fact, she was downright miserable. She sniffed again. No doubt she'd get over it. In a hundred years or so.

She hadn't seen Rafe again after their horrible meeting yesterday morning. Somehow she hadn't expected that when she walked out. Some tiny, stupid part of her had really thought he'd come after her.

Crazy or what?

Last night she'd waited for him to come home. Not knowing what she would say, but needing to see him so badly she hurt.

Eventually, she'd asked Charles, who'd been casting disapproving glances in her direction ever since she'd gotten home yesterday afternoon. Except it wasn't her home. It was Rafe's house.

Charles had informed her that Rafe had requested a bag be packed and sent to his office. He'd taken the company jet and gone to New York. Charles had made it sound as though this early departure was all her fault. And maybe he was right.

Today she'd worked well into the evening, showing tourists the sites of London, and had managed to keep busy and not wallow in too much self-pity. But when she got back to the empty house, the sense of loneliness had almost swamped her. Poor Toby had sensed her mood and done his best to cheer her up, but it just wasn't happening. And Charles wasn't helping. He'd hardly said a word to her, but his critical glares had made her squirm. She hadn't done anything wrong. Had she?

This was self-preservation.

In the end, she'd hidden herself away in the wine cellar, opened a bottle of red, and was now slumped on the floor, back against the wall, legs stretched out in front of her, looking at paperwork for properties in San Sebastian. While SA International would provide her with accommodations for the month she was in London, she was expected to find her own place for the year in Spain. She couldn't concentrate. Couldn't imagine herself in any of the places.

"He's flown away, Toby. You're all I have left." Toby put his front paws on her thighs, stretched up, and licked her face.

The words blurred, and she screwed up the papers and tossed them on the floor.

"Maybe we should join the army instead? Go shoot something." She patted Toby on the head. "You can be a sniffer dog."

It was after midnight. She should go to bed. But she'd packed her bags, and they were sitting on the floor in her bedroom, and she couldn't face looking at them right now. It hurt too much. What was she going to do? What if Rafe decided he didn't want to be friends with her anymore and she never saw him again?

"He's a bad man, Toby. He promised Gary he'd look after me and instead he broke my heart."

Someone cleared their throat and she jumped. Oh God, Charles. Had he heard her confessing her broken heart to a dog?

He appeared around the corner of a wine rack. "Mrs. Sinclair."

"Bella," she said automatically, as she had done every time he called her that.

"Bella," he conceded. That was a first. "I brought you a glass for the wine."

"Aw, how sweet. But I'm okay with the bottle." She picked it up and hugged it to her chest.

"Then perhaps I might have a glass." He held it out, and she eyed him suspiciously.

"You think I've had enough, don't you? You think I'm a bad influence on Toby."

"Yes."

She snorted but patted the floor beside her. "Sit down, and I'll give you some."

He pursed his lips, but he came down beside her. She filled his glass and sat back. "You've known Rafe all his life, haven't you?" He nodded. "Tell me what he was like as a little boy."

Charles took a sip of his wine. "He was…perfect."

She sighed. "I should have guessed." Why couldn't he have been just a little bit of a mess?

• • •

Rafe paused before the door. Through it drifted the sounds of music and subdued conversation. A wave of exhaustion washed over him. At the best of times, he didn't like parties.

He'd thought about not making the trip, but he'd needed to put some distance between him and Bella. Otherwise he might have gone begging. And he couldn't face any more rejection right now. He also needed to talk to his mother. The sort of conversation that couldn't be done over the phone. Tell her he was about to reveal the family secret. That should make her birthday special.

He doubted the truth would make any difference to Bella. He still wouldn't be able to give her what she needed. But at least she would understand why.

What would she be doing now? It was three in the morning back in London. She'd be asleep. Was she lying in bed dreaming about him? Doubtful.

He exhaled and then pushed open the doors. The room was huge, surrounded by glass walls, and all around them the lights of New York sparkled. But not as much as the people inside. All glittering and perfect. At least on the surface. Like him.

He couldn't see his mother, and he made his way across to the bar. A few people murmured greetings as he passed, but something about his mood tonight must have warned them off, because they didn't pause to talk.

"Whiskey," he said to the barman.

He gulped down the first and held out his glass for a refill. He was on his third, the alcohol a buzz in his head, when someone sat at the barstool next to him. Rafe glanced up. It was John, his lawyer, probably one of the few people who would risk approaching him in this mood.

"How's the baby-making going?" John asked.

"Fuck off."

"That well, huh?" He peered around. "So where is she? I

take it she's here tonight."

Rafe shrugged. "She didn't want to come."

"To the most celebrated party in the New York social calendar?"

"Bella's not like that."

"Well, your mother will be disappointed. She was grilling me earlier on your new girlfriend." When he didn't answer, John continued, "Of course I told her my lips were sealed."

Rafe had never doubted for a moment that John would keep quiet about his arrangement with Bella.

"Tell me," John murmured, "did Bella really tell your sister she was having your baby?"

"Not exactly."

At that moment, he caught sight of his mother's blond hair through the crowd. Without saying anything else, he placed his empty glass on the bar, got to his feet, and headed over. His gut tightened with every step. His mother was not going to take this well. He hated to hurt her, but he could no longer keep quiet. Not to Bella.

As he halted by the small group of people, they parted to allow Rafe to greet his mother. She looked as beautiful as ever, her hair and makeup perfect. Bending toward her, he kissed her cheek. "Mother, happy birthday." He reached into his pocket and pulled out a flat gift-wrapped box.

His mother took the package and clutched it in her hand. "Rafe, are you alone?"

"Yes."

"Could I talk to you for a moment? Somewhere quiet."

"Of course." They definitely needed quiet for what he had to say.

He followed his mother into a small room off the main ballroom. Closing the door behind them, he turned and faced her.

Her hands were clenched in front of her. "Gina said—"

"I've a good idea what she said," he interrupted. "And no, Bella is not pregnant."

Her shoulders slumped. "But you're seeing her. And it's serious?"

"Yes."

"Have you told her about…?" she asked.

"No. But I plan to."

"Why?" A hint of panic laced her voice. "When you've never told anyone else?"

"Because she deserves to know the reason I can't marry her, give her a family."

Her hand flew to her chest, and she sank down onto the chair behind her. Rafe crossed to where a table held a decanter and glasses. He poured them both a drink, then handed her one. She took the glass and perched on the edge of the chair. Finally, she took a deep breath. "You love her?"

"Yes, but it will never work between us. She wants children."

"I'm sorry. But there are ways…"

He knew there were ways. Just not for him right now. Bella had said she would wait. But for how long? He couldn't ask her to wait indefinitely.

"I haven't been able to stop thinking about this since your sister told me what Bella said…about the baby." His mother interrupted his thoughts. "All these years, I've managed to ignore it."

His heart sank as he realized his mother was on some sort of guilt trip. Again.

"All those years ago, I should have questioned why Miguel was ill." She took a sip of her drink. "But I've always hated illness, and I just pretended it wasn't happening. And when he left me, I truly believed it was because we wanted different things."

"Instead he was going home to die."

"Yes."

In the past, his mother had only ever talked about his father when it was absolutely necessary. Rafe knew now that it wasn't disinterest, but guilt. "Would it have made a difference if you'd known?" he asked.

She jumped to her feet, knocking her glass so it shattered on the marble floor. They both ignored it.

"I don't know. I still can't believe Miguel didn't tell me. I believed he didn't care enough to stay and try to work things through. Instead, he thought I wasn't strong enough, that maybe I wouldn't love him enough to stand by him, and all I could do was go on about how I wanted more babies."

Rafe crossed the room and poured her another drink. It occurred to him the similarities between his situation and his father's. Except perhaps that was being unfair to Bella. She was a much stronger character than his mother.

He still loved his mother—that's why he had tried so hard to be what she wanted. The perfect son. But no more. He was ready to smash that image to pieces.

"Sit down," he said, handing her the glass.

She took it and sank onto the sofa. Rafe sat beside her and took her free hand. "He didn't tell you. You couldn't have known."

"Yes, but if I'd been a different person maybe he would have risked telling me. And I can't help thinking that if he'd stayed in London, he might have gotten better medical treatment. He might still be alive."

She went silent, and Rafe sat back, leaning his head against the sofa. She might be right. Maybe something could have been done to save him. Rafe had researched the disease that had killed his father. The disease he carried in his genes that had overshadowed his life from a time when he was too young to understand the full consequences. But telling her that now would hardly help. As she'd pointed out, she'd never been good around illness. Rafe had learned at an early age to keep away from her if he felt less than well. Then again, she'd stuck with his stepfather through cancer.

"When your grandfather told me after the funeral what had really happened, I was devastated. And that you might be..." She downed the rest of her drink. "I wasn't very supportive. But I was in shock."

She'd sent him for the tests, and when they'd come back positive, she'd never mentioned the subject again. His grandfather had talked to him about it. But his mother had made him feel as though it was a secret to be locked away. So he had.

"I should have talked to you about it. Instead, I made you hide it as though it was something to be ashamed of. But it was me who was ashamed. Ashamed of what people would think if they knew, and if they knew about Miguel and that I hadn't stood by him. And I was so scared you would get ill."

"There was never any chance of that," Rafe said.

"Maybe. But I just couldn't enjoy my party without talking to you about it."

"Well, now we have. Why don't you go back? They'll be missing you."

"I think I will. I feel better now." She put down her glass and frowned. "You're still going to tell her?"

"Yes. But don't worry. Bella won't reveal our secret to anyone else."

She gave a quick nod, her expression clearing. "Of course not."

When she'd gone, he stood, wandered over to the window, and stared at the city. He was scared. Scared Bella would reject him. That he didn't deserve her anyway. She thought he was perfect, and he was as far from perfect as was possible. He was flawed at such a basic level.

Through his childhood he had sought his mother's

approval, and even as an adult, he'd done the same, always ensuring he presented the illusion of flawlessness. He could see his reflection in the glass, and he reached up and ran a hand through his hair. He tugged his tie loose and opened his collar. He didn't want to be perfect.

He was leaving his mother's glittering idea of perfection. He'd go back to London, tell Bella his secrets, and see if she'd accept the less-than-perfect person he really was.

He was headed for the door when his cell phone rang.

Chapter Fourteen

A light touch on her arm dragged her from sleep.

She was in Rafe's bed, hugging his pillow to her breasts. She shoved it away, rolled over, and blinked. Daylight filtered through the curtains, but she could tell it was still early. A figure loomed over her.

Charles. What the hell?

"Mrs. Sinclair."

She yawned, then pulled herself up. Toby's nose appeared from beneath the sheet, and Charles didn't even complain. Something was wrong.

Her breath caught in her throat, and her chest tightened. "What is it? Is it Rafe?"

"He's fine," he said soothingly. "He just phoned. There's been an incident in Spain. He wanted me to talk to you in case you heard from anyone else."

She frowned. "What sort of incident?"

"A fire."

Fires were a yearly hazard she'd learned to live with. They were usually doused quickly and efficiently, but occasionally one would get out of control with devastating consequences.

"Oh my God. How's his grandfather?"

"Apparently the fire didn't touch the villa. But he was trying to help fight it and collapsed from the smoke. They think he might have had another heart attack."

Poor Rafe. "How is he?"

"He's alive. That's all Mr. Sanchez knows right now. But there's something else."

A cold feeling of dread filled her. "What is it?"

"Your house. It was totally destroyed in the fire."

• • •

It was hours later when Rafe's plane landed. They were doing a fast turnaround and heading for Spain, so she was taken straightaway to board.

She climbed the stairs and peered into the body of the plane, wary of seeing Rafe after their last meeting, but wanting to go to him so badly it hurt. She still wasn't able to take it in. The whole thing seemed unreal.

Right in front of her was a comfortable seating area, with soft leather couches around a coffee table. Beyond that was a section with rows of chairs like a normal plane. Rafe sat in one of the aisle seats, working on a laptop, but he glanced up as she approached.

He appeared tired, dark circles under his eyes, cheeks shadowed. His perfect image was unraveling. She came to a halt in front of him, leaned down, and hugged him, pulling his head against her. His arms wrapped around her waist, and for long moments she stood holding him close, breathing in the familiar scent of him. For the first time since she'd heard about the fire, her mind stopped spinning and she felt at peace.

"Readying for takeoff." The words came over the

speakers, and reluctantly, she pulled herself free, took her seat beside him, and fastened the belt.

She closed her eyes as the plane took off, stayed that way until they leveled out. Neither of them had spoken yet; now she turned to Rafe. "It doesn't matter," she said. "About the house, I mean. As long as your grandfather recovers, the rest isn't important."

But she wasn't sure she was being truthful. The thought of the home she'd shared with Gary, the love they'd put into restoring the place, all turned to ashes, caused an ache in her heart. But that had to come second to Rafe's grandfather. She'd never known whether it was duty or love that made Rafe visit the old man in Spain. Now she could see the news had shattered him.

"You love him, don't you?" she said.

"He was the only one who saw me as I really am and loved me anyway. And in return, I avoided him and the place as much as I could, because he reminded me of what I was."

She frowned at his words. There was more here than just the heart attack. She rested her hand on his arm. The muscles were rigid with tension. "Tell me," she said.

He shook his head. "Not now. Later, I'll tell you everything." His cell phone rang and he picked it up, listened for a minute, and some of the tension eased from his features. He ended the call and leaned his head back against the seat. "That was the doctor. He's awake and fine and asking for wine."

A smile tugged her lips. The first in a while. "I'm glad."

He sat up, looked at her. "Will you come and lie with me? It seems like an age since I slept and…"

She nodded.

Without waiting for an answer, he took her by the shoulders and pulled her out of her chair and into his lap. His mouth came down on hers in a gentle kiss. Then he kissed her cheeks and her eyelids, butterfly kisses that sent heat coursing through her.

"Make love with me," he murmured against her skin.

The muscles in her belly contracted at his words, but before she could answer, he shifted her in his lap and then rose to his feet. He strode through the cabin with her in his arms, kicking open the door at the rear. It led into a bedroom with a huge bed in the center that took up almost the entire width of the plane.

Rafe lowered her gently to the mattress, then stood over her as he stripped the clothes from his body. The sight lodged any words in her throat. Bella couldn't have told him no—even if she'd wanted to. Which she didn't.

He peeled her clothes from her body, kissing each part as it was revealed to him. By the time he lay naked beside her, she was shaking. "Please, Rafe."

"Patience," he murmured, dropping a slow kiss on her breast, sending darts of fire down to her groin.

His teeth grazed her throat. He kissed each nipple, his mouth hot and wet, then moved lower, and his lips pressed against her stomach. His hot breath ruffled the curls at the base of her belly, sending frissons of sensation skittering across her skin. Everything tightened inside her until she was coiled taut with anticipation, her heart racing, a pulse throbbing between her thighs.

He parted her legs with his free hand, spreading them, leaving her open to him. She held her breath, squeezed her eyes tightly shut as he hovered over her, teasing her with his warm, velvet tongue. He devoured her, his hot mouth bringing every nerve in her body to life, adrenaline spiking in her blood, her hips jerking upward against his lips. His tongue stroked against her swollen clit, and the ability to think deserted her. Arching her back, she pushed her sex against him, needing more. He sucked the sensitive nub into his mouth and she came, stars flashing behind her tightly closed lids.

Afterward, he crawled up her body and took her with exquisite gentleness, his gaze holding hers as he slowly pushed deeper inside, filling her totally. Bella lay beneath him, heart throbbing as the languid thrust of his body urged her upward. Wrapping her legs around his waist, her hands clung to his broad shoulders as he drove her higher, his every movement controlled, filled with leashed power.

She was throbbing with need by the time they came together and pleasure exploded inside her, arching her back as she called out his name.

He held her close as tremors shivered through her, then kissed her mouth.

Words hovered on her lips, and she swallowed them. She burrowed her head against his shoulder and allowed the caress of his hands to sooth her to sleep.

He was still holding her when she awoke, and she shifted in his arms so she could look down into his face. He was awake, watching her. "Thank you."

"There's no need," she said. "I wanted you."

"Charles told me you were packed. You're still leaving?"

"I don't have a choice. Not if you won't talk to me."

He gave a bitter smile. "I'll talk to you. I doubt what I have to say will change your mind, though. But later. Right now, we're coming in to land. If you want to clean up there's a shower through there." He nodded to the back of the cabin.

When she came out of the bathroom ten minutes later, Rafe was gone, and she dressed quickly and went back into the main cabin.

A car drove them from the airport to the villa. It was late afternoon in Spain by the time they arrived. Rafe's grandfather was sleeping, but the doctor thought he'd wake soon.

"Did he not need to go to hospital?" Rafe asked.

The doctor shrugged. "You know how he is, he wouldn't even consider it. Besides, it was a very minor attack, and you probably have more equipment here than the local surgery."

"I'll wait with him until he wakes." Rafe sank into the chair beside the bed.

Bella went across and rested a hand on his shoulder. "I'm going to go look at the house."

He glanced up, concern in his eyes. "Are you sure you want to go alone?"

"I'll be all right."

"I'll meet you there after I've spoken with him."

Outside the gates of the villa, a black line showed where the fire had stopped. So close. Beyond that, the vegetation was charred, the trees burned to the ground, and the stench of stale smoke and ashes hung in the air.

She took the familiar path from the villa to the farmhouse, nausea gripping her stomach as she got closer to the farm. When she turned the final corner, her breath caught. The house was totally destroyed, a blackened shell. She approached slowly and peered through the empty front doorway. Nothing could be salvaged. The fire must have roared through so quickly.

Everything was lost. She'd taken very little with her to London—she'd left all the keepsakes of Gary's and her life together behind.

But in a sudden blinding insight, she realized it didn't matter. Her memories were what were important, and she would never lose them, never forget what Gary had brought to her life. The house was just a pile a bricks. It hadn't been a home since he'd died. She'd have realized that sooner if she hadn't been so stubborn.

Homes were made up of people, not places.

She turned away from the house. The main building was destroyed, but the outbuildings still stood. She crossed the charred lawn and peered through the door of Gary's workshop. The cradle stood where she'd left it, still perfect. She thought of the little blue-eyed baby who might never be. But the thought didn't hurt as much as she'd expected.

Rafe cared for her, maybe even loved her. Despite their differences, or maybe even because of them. She had no clue what he was going to tell her. But it was something big. Something he believed would change the way she felt about him—did he think her so shallow?

He'd always been her friend, but over the weeks they'd been together, he had grown to be far, far more. Her friend, her lover, her chance for a future. She wanted to run to him. Tell him she loved him, and that for her, home was wherever he was.

In the end, though, she didn't return to the villa. She found a notebook in her bag, scribbled a note, and tacked it to the workshop door.

Then headed up the track behind the ruined house.

• • •

His grandfather had awoken and was as stubborn as ever, refusing to even consider going into hospital. Instead, the doctor had hired a nurse so he'd have around-the-clock attention. He would be fine; the old man was tough.

Rafe left him to sleep and headed out to find Bella, coming to an abrupt halt as he caught sight of the ruins of her home. He moved closer, but all was quiet.

"Bella?"

No answer.

He shouldn't have let her come alone. First, she'd lost Gary, and now this. She was probably totally devastated, not thinking straight. Where would she go?

He glanced in through what had been the front door, but Bella wasn't inside. He turned, searching the area for some sign. Gary's workshop was still in good condition, and he wandered over and saw the note on the door.

He ripped it free, read the words.

Gone swimming.

Crumpling the note, he shoved it in his pocket. Then headed up the steep track at the back of the house.

Chapter Fifteen

She was seated on the bank, her legs dangling in the water, her eyes closed. Rafe stood for a minute and watched her, his chest tightening. She'd given herself so sweetly and so completely on the plane. How could he let her go?

As though sensing him, she blinked and turned her head as he stepped out of the shadow of the trees.

"I used to come here when I was a boy," he said. "It was the one place I loved, but I never expected to find my own dryad here. That first time, I thought I'd dreamed you up, that you were some magical creature."

"I'm real."

"I know. I knew then. Maybe it was wishful thinking. Maybe if you weren't real, I was allowed to touch you…kiss you."

"You were allowed anyway."

He shook his head. "I'd been fighting so hard, for so long, not to think of you that way."

"And did you succeed?"

"You know I didn't. One look and I was lost. I want you

now more than I ever did."

"You can have me, Rafe. I'm yours."

Blood sank to his groin at the words, and for a moment he was tempted. Just one more time. He sighed and ran a hand through his already-ruffled hair. "We have to talk."

"I know." She patted the sand beside her. "Come sit with me."

He sank down onto the ground, positioning himself so he could watch her face. How to begin? "I've never spoken of this to anyone before, but my father didn't die of pneumonia as my mother always told people. He died of a blood disease that's been in our family for generations."

Her eyes widened, and she reached out a hand to him. "Are you ill?"

"I'm fine. I never had the disease." He picked up her hand and toyed with her fingers, rubbing his thumb over her palm. "But I am a carrier."

"What does that mean?"

"It means I could pass it on to any children I have."

Her hand flew to her chest. "Oh. That's why…?"

He nodded. Now that he'd started, he needed to purge this from his system. "My grandfather is a carrier like me, though a bit more so. My grandmother had the disease. It's prevalent in the area, all around the Mediterranean actually, but back then people didn't really understand it. My grandmother had numerous miscarriages and stillbirths before my father was born. The baby after him killed her."

"Your poor grandfather."

At least she wasn't recoiling in horror. All he could see in her face was sympathy. "He doesn't talk about it much—it hurts too badly. Anyway, my father was fine growing up. I think Grandfather hoped it had passed him by and put off telling him—he'd thought he could leave it until he decided to marry. And then my mother became pregnant."

Her eyes were bright with unshed tears. She blinked and dashed them away with the back of her hand. He hated that he'd made her sad.

"You're sure you're not ill? You won't suddenly get sick?" She swallowed. "Is this disease treatable?"

"It can't be cured, but there are things that can be done to control it, blood transfusions, other things. But there's no risk I'll get it."

"Whew." She gave a weak smile, then chewed on her lip. "It's not *so* bad, then."

He closed his eyes for a second, a sensation of lightness washing over him. Why had he ever believed she would turn from him? He searched her face, trying to analyze what she was feeling. Sympathy, hope, maybe more...

He needed to touch her, and he cupped her cheek in his hand, stroking her soft skin with the pad of his thumb. Leaning across, he kissed her lightly on the lips. "I wish my mother had been more like you. I grew up thinking it was some dark, horrible secret I couldn't talk about. Not even to Gary. I know now I built it up into more than it was, let it have too much control over me."

She squeezed his fingers. "I think you're perfect."

"Nobody's perfect." He sighed. "I was going to come back to London and ask you to marry me," he said. "After the party. I was going to tell you all this first, and then ask you."

She opened her mouth to reply, but he hurried on, needing to get everything out in the open. Scared of what she might say. "I've been having some research done. So far it's not good news, and I can't *promise* you the children you want. I always swore I would never have children, never risk passing this on. I swore to myself it would end with me, but I know what having a family means to you"—he took a deep breath—"and I'll do everything I can to give you that family. There have been a lot of advances in gene manipulation over the last couple of decades, and they're finding new methods all the time."

His heart was racing, and he studied their joined hands, twining her fingers with his. "And I've already contacted a contractor about rebuilding your house. He'll start right away, make it exactly as it was. If you want to live here, we can."

"You hate it here."

His gaze shot to her face, where a little frown was forming between her eyes. "I'll cope, if you're here with me. Or if you still want to take that job—then we can move to San Sebastian."

She shook her head. "You'd do that for me?"

"I'd do anything for you. Anything I can," he added, because he still couldn't give her what she really wanted. Would it be enough?

When she remained silent, he forced himself to go on. "You don't have to say anything right now. You need to think about what I've said. What you want." But there was one more thing he had to say. The most important thing. Because none of what he'd said mattered, not without this.

He took a deep, steadying breath and said the words he hoped she wanted to hear. "I love you."

The world stopped as he waited for her to say something. Anything.

Instead, she tugged her hand free and rose to her feet. His heart stopped beating. Had he lost after all?

Then holding his gaze, she slowly stripped the clothes from her body. He couldn't move as each beautiful, familiar curve was revealed. By the time she stood before him naked, he was breathing fast. The blood throbbed in his veins, sinking to his groin, making him hot and hard. She turned, and with a last glance over her shoulder, she dived into the water.

He closed his eyes briefly and exhaled.

Madre de dios. Thank you.

His hands fumbled as he dragged the clothes from his body, excitement making him clumsy. Finally, he lowered himself into the pool beside her. Reaching for her, he drew her close.

Resting her hands on his shoulders, she looked up into his face, her eyes filled with desire and more.

Say it. Say it.

"I love you," she said.

The air left his lungs. It was enough. The words would last him through whatever came next.

He kissed her gently, then harder. He'd never get enough. Finally, he had to breathe. "I love you."

"How long?" she asked. "How long have you loved me?"

"From the moment I met you."

His hands slid down under the water to circle her waist, and then lower to cup her ass and draw her closer. "I dreamed of this so many times," he said. "Dreamed of the night we first kissed, and in my dreams it always ended here with you in my arms."

"I dreamed as well. And my dreams brought me to this place. With you."

Rafe lowered his head and kissed her, giving himself up to the feeling of rightness, of coming home. They moved together without conscious thought and soon were joined as one.

"I love you." The words were torn from his throat as he stiffened, shuddering inside her, then he was kissing her again, devouring her.

Afterward, he pulled her out of the water and they lay on the sandy bank for a long time, her arms wrapped tight around him. Above them, the sun descended and the stars came out. Finally, she pulled free of his arms and sat up. "Rafe, will you marry me?"

For a second, shock held him still, then his lips curled into a huge grin he couldn't seem to control. *"Si, querida."*

"Good. That's settled then."

Still, he had to be sure. "Have you thought it through? What it could mean? I know all you wanted was a home, a family. You might not get that."

"I have thought, and I want children, but I want you more. The whole you, with whatever problems you bring along. From now on, my home will always be where you are."

"We'll have a family, *querida*. Somehow, I'll give you everything you've always wanted."

She shook her head. "Don't make promises. Don't make our lives about that one thing."

"You know, if they'd known more in the past, then my grandparents would never have married. It's crazy—if they'd only understood more, so much heartbreak could have been avoided."

"And your father would never have existed. You would never have existed. I'm glad they didn't know. Besides, maybe your grandfather loved her and would have married her anyway."

"Maybe."

"I like to think so." She leaned across, cupped his face in her hands. "You're all I want. All I'll ever want."

He slid his hand beneath her hair and pulled her closer. "Then kiss me, *querida*. Kiss me like you did that night. Like you'll never, ever get enough of me."

And she did.

Epilogue

"He's perfect," Mark said.

Bella reached down and stroked the soft skin of her baby's cheek. "He is," she murmured.

And he was perfect in every way. She would have loved him anyway, but she was glad for Rafe's sake that Miguel was totally free of the disease that had killed Rafe's father.

Despite her telling Rafe not to worry, he'd poured endless energy, not to mention money, into finding a solution, and Miguel was the result. Having vast amounts of money did come in useful sometimes. But the research would be used for all sufferers of the disease, would help countless lives.

Miguel was three months old, and they had just had the christening. Now they were back at the house in Belgravia, and Miguel lay in the cradle Gary had carved for their baby. Rafe had had it brought from Spain for her. She hadn't thought she could love him any more.

Mark was godfather, handsome in his uniform. And all

Rafe's family was present, including his grandfather—the first time he had left Spain.

Rafe came up beside her and slipped his hands around her waist, pulling her against him. He tugged her backward into the hallway, away from the guests, and turned her in his arms, pressing her up against the wood-paneled wall.

Looping her hand around his neck, she pulled him down toward her. "Kiss me," she murmured.

And he did.

Acknowledgments

A huge thank you to everyone at Entangled Publishing for persevering with my Spaniard. And to all the great women at Passionate Critters for reading my stories and letting me know what they really think. And finally, to my husband Rob, who puts up with me, and encourages me, and does a great job of hiding it when he's totally fed up with me vanishing into my imaginary worlds and filling the house with imaginary people.

About the Author

Nina Croft grew up in the north of England. After training as an accountant, she spent four years working as a volunteer in Zambia, which left her with a love of the sun and a dislike of nine-to-five work. She then spent a number of years mixing travel (whenever possible) with work (whenever necessary) but has now settled down to a life of writing and picking almonds on a remote farm in the mountains of southern Spain.

Nina writes all types of romance, often mixed with elements of the paranormal and science fiction.

If you'd like to have learn about new releases sign up for Nina's newsletter here: http://eepurl.com/rZ5rz

www.ninacroft.com

THE ORDER SERIES

BITTERSWEET BLOOD
BITTERSWEET MAGIC
BITTERSWEET DARKNESS
BITTERSWEET CHRISTMAS
THE ORDER BOXED SET

THE BEYOND HUMAN SERIES

UNTHINKABLE
UNSPEAKABLE
UNCONTROLLABLE

THE MELVILLE SISTERS SERIES

OPERATION SAVING DANIEL
BETTING ON JULIA

THE SADDLER COVE SERIES

HANDLE WITH CARE

THE RUBY ROBBINS' SEXY SPACE ODYSSEY SERIES

RESCUED BY THE SPACE PIRATE
STOLEN BY THE SPACE PIRATE
SAVING THE SPACE PIRATE

HEART AND SOLE
a novel by Miranda Liasson

Maddie Kingston just walked away from everything in order to take over her family's struggling shoe business. Unfortunately, the majority of the company's shares have been bought out by none other than Maddie's ex-boyfriend, billionaire Nick Holter. Now Maddie needs his help, even if even if it means buying Nick from a charity bachelor auction. Between their families' feud and their own unfinished business, tempers—and emotions—run hot. *Too* hot. Because kissing with the enemy is a guaranteed shoe-in for trouble...

THE BILLIONAIRE'S CHRISTMAS BABY
a novel by Victoria James

A baby on the doorstep is the least of Hannah Woods's problems—she has to find the baby's uncle, or the child will end up in foster care. She sleuths her way to the reclusive CEO's doorstep only to find six feet of holiday sexy—and a door slammed in her face. But when Jackson comes around and urges they marry for little Emily's sake, Hannah finds herself falling for the jaded billionaire and wishing for a holiday miracle of their own...

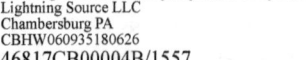